The War Chest

contained over a million dollars in gold—California's contribution to Lincoln's war.

It was Captain Jeff Marshak's urgent mission to carry it from the coast to the Capital. When his detachment died in ambush and their replacements were slaughtered in an Apache massacre, the Captain was left with a bloody fortune and an ungrateful survivor. Her name was Marcie Denton, and she had already brought him to court martial charges; now she had to help him bluff his way to Washington.

All he needed was a hand of iron, an unsleeping eye, and a miracle to get him through the Hell Road.

The Hell Road

by RAY HOGAN

A SIGNET BOOK from
NEW AMERICAN LIBRARY
TIMES MIRROR

PUBLISHED BY
THE NEW AMERICAN LIBRARY
OF CANADA LIMITED

First Signet Printing, October, 1968

2 3 4 5 6 7 8 9

SIGNET TRADEMARK REG. U.S. PAT. OFF. AND FOREIGN COUNTRIES
REGISTERED TRADEMARK — MARCA REGISTRADA
HECHO EN WINNIPEG, CANADA

SIGNET, SIGNET CLASSICS, MENTOR, PLUME AND MERIDIAN BOOKS are published in Canada by The New American Library of Canada Limited, Scarborough, Ontario

PRINTED IN CANADA

COVER PRINTED IN U.S.A.

. . . for my wife, LOIS

1

Where the hell was Fort Whiterock?

Jeff Marshak, the strident yells of Apaches lashing him from all quarters, braced himself in the careening wagon, dashed sweat from his eyes. Taking a tighter grip on the reins, clutching his rifle with the other, he strained to see beyond the bobbing heads of the wildly galloping mules. Nothing. . . . Only sand, shallow arroyos, low, rolling hills, and empty sky. But Whiterock was out there—somewhere.

At his feet the body of Amos Miller thumped against his shins like an erratic drumbeat. The bearded old sergeant had been the first of the seven-man escort to die. After that, the Indians had picked the others off, one by one; now, he was the sole remaining member of the party.

A lance sailed through the dust-clogged air, making an odd swishing sound in its passage. The tip of the blade grazed the rump of the off-mule, sent him lunging against his collar. Instantly the wagon slewed to the side, skidded down into a dry watercourse on two wheels, righted itself and bounced up the opposite bank.

The yelling increased as the Apaches began to sweep in nearer, hungering for the final kill. There were a dozen or so of them yet—some naked except for breechcloths, a few in dirty white shirts and drawers, and all with strips of cloth around their head.

A muscular young buck, bronze body glistening in the streaming sunlight, lips drawn back in a snarl, swerved in on Marshak's left. Legs clamped to the heaving flanks of his pony, he bent low, aimed an arrow. Marshak fired hurriedly. The bullet smashed into the Apache's chest, knocked him from his mount. It was the Henry that was keeping him alive, Jeff realized. The new repeating rifle's facility for continuous firing without reloading puzzled the Indians, filled them with awe and a reluctance to venture close.

Again he shook off the sweat; he wouldn't be able to hold out much longer despite his weapon and a determination to get through. A bullet splintered into the seat rest. He swore angrily. He'd been lucky in one respect. The Apaches were armed with only a few rifles and with those weren't very adept. Otherwise he'd be dead like Miller and Rudd and Ambrose Kinnerman—and all the others.

He felt a stab of pain in his left arm, glanced down. An arrow hung loosely from the flesh above his elbow. He jerked himself violently, the shaft pulled loose, fell. Apaches were swarming all around him, yelling, screeching, their dark, paint-smeared faces contorted with hate.

He saw a flash deep in the center of a smoke puff as a brave fired from almost point-blank range. The swaying jolting of the wagon saved him. An arrow thunked into the dashboard, stood there quivering; a second buried itself in Miller's body. Again a rifle blasted from nearby. A slug ripped through his hat.

He was fighting to keep the mules under control, striving to prevent them from overturning the wagon in their frantic haste. The vehicle swung broadside again, began to tip in its skid. Marshak dropped the Henry to the floor, grabbed at the seat rail to keep from being thrown out as the wagon started whipping back and forth.

The yelling increased as the painted warriors closed in. He wasn't going to make it—he could see that. There were just too damned many of them—and the magazine of the Henry was almost empty.

Something struck him a glancing blow on the head. He shook himself savagely, throwing off the momentary daze. Sheer reflex brought him around. An Apache had gained a foothold on the wagon, was clinging to the back of the seat with one hand, held aloft a flint knife with the other. Jeff jerked to one side, reached. His fingers closed about the brave's wrist. He yanked hard and the Apache fell, going down under the wheel.

Another was riding hard on the right, trying to get a foot's purchase on the sideboard near the seat. Marshak snatched up the Henry, jammed the muzzle into the man's belly, and pulled the trigger. The Indian flung backward, his howls lost in the rattling and popping of the wagon.

And then the Apaches began to fade in the dust. Fresh

gunshots broke out from a rise dead ahead. An irregular line of blue-clad cavalrymen was flowing down the grade—and beyond them a scatter of low-roofed buildings, huts and sun-bleached tents appeared on the horizon. Jeff Marshak grinned wolfishly and hauled back on the sweat-soaked leather ribbons gripped tight in his hands. . . . Fort Whiterock—at last.

From the moment they entered the southwest corner of New Mexico Territory, Marshak was uneasy. Reports had reached him when they crossed the Colorado that the Apaches, for some reason, were again on the prowl, attacking travelers, raiding settlements and ranches with increasing boldness.

Added to that was the danger from Mexican *bandidos,* taking advantage of the disturbances to violate the border and prey on the wagon trains and the few coaches still making their way to and from California.

He'd circumvented that last possibility to some extent by keeping his party well north of the line since the Mexicans feared to venture too deep onto American soil, and so far they'd seen nothing of outlaws. But it was different where the Apaches were concerned. It was said they could be expected everywhere.

But it was not until several mornings later when he caught sight of a small group riding tight-bunched a quarter mile to the south. They appeared to be going nowhere in particular, simply cruising along, maintaining pace. He'd taken immediate precautions.

"Kennerman!" he called, and waved in the leathery-faced corporal. "Put the men three to a side—no more than twenty paces apart. Want them close to the wagon."

"Yes, sir," Kennerman said, saluting, and wheeled away, bawling instructions to the remaining troopers.

"If we're going to get hit," Marshak said to Miller, hunched beside him on the seat, "they ought to be where they can do some good."

The old noncom, testy and squint-eyed from years of desert duty, shifted his cud. Gauging the distance to the off-front wheel, he splattered and sand-polished steel tire with brown.

"Ain't nothing helping much if a big bunch takes a notion to crack down on us," he said dourly. "Apaches is plain hell."

Marshak shrugged, fingered the hammer of his Henry rifle. He'd been able to obtain only one of the new repeaters for the journey, they were in such short supply; he had kept it for his own use. *One man with a Henry's as good as a whole squad,* so went the saying. Best position for such a weapon, he thus reasoned, was on the wagon.

"When you figure we'll be reaching Whiterock, Cap'n?" Miller asked, again desecrating the wheel.

"Soon, according to the map. Before the day's over, I'd guess."

"Maps ain't worth a goddamn, mostly," Miller said with an enlistee's fine disdain. "Made by jaspers who ain't never seen the country—usually."

Jeff Marshak agreed silently. So far, the map provided by Carleton's adjutant had been wrong on about every count. He'd see if he couldn't get better directions once they reached Fort Whiterock.

Lids pulled down to minimize the searing glare, he stared moodily at the scarred land stretched before him in gray emptiness. Shimmering heat waves danced in endless procession, wilting even the cholla and catclaw, and in the distance a mass of shadowy mountains tumbled in low, ragged confusion across the horizon. Whiterock would lie somewhere near those hills, he supposed.

He swung his glance around. Kennerman had the troopers properly spaced. The corporal rode in the lead to the right, followed by Wills and Peter Bucknell. On the opposite side of the wagon Noah Rudd was out front. Behind him came Ross Conroy and then the new recruit, Wade Krause. Frowning, Jeff started to hail Kennerman, to have Krause moved to the center of the short line. He didn't like the man, but Krause, being green, would be better off in the middle.

He shrugged off the thought. It didn't matter. If the Apaches came swarming in out of nowhere, as they usually did, jumped them fast, it wouldn't make much difference where a man rode.

Idly, he wondered why he'd taken a dislike to Krause, reckoned it was the man's face; narrow, sly, with shifty shoe-button eyes. Marshak stirred with self-disgust. A hell of a thing to judge a man by. He'd been that route himself. A New Yorker, born of Polish immigrants, his climb up through the ranks had been a rough one—due mostly to just such groundless discrimination.

No place for foreigners on the roll of commissioned officers, had seemed to be an unwritten law. Well, he'd broken their rule for them and made them like it. He'd clawed his way to a captaincy, and he wasn't finished yet, even though there had been those with good connections who'd managed to get him transferred to remote California, the end of the world insofar as Washington was concerned.

He hadn't really minded. He was living the life he liked, and when opportunity came along in the form of delivering the California War Chest, he had gone to General Carleton and volunteered for the job, seeing in it not only a break in the usual post routine but a means for being of real service to the uniform.

That had been more than three weeks ago—three weeks and they were barely started on the long journey to Washington. If he didn't—

"Cap'n," Miller said, "you figure they's a chance we can get into this war—if it starts?"

"It's started," Marshak replied, "but a far piece from here. Likely never see a Reb this far west."

"Hell of a note," the noncom grumbled. "Man pounds his butt on a saddle half his life learning how to fight, then never gets close enough to use it."

"They're the Apaches—the others—"

"Different kind of fighting. I mean a real war. Artillery and cannon and such."

Marshak smiled. "Well, don't give up altogether. May find things a mite hot when we get to Missouri."

"Thought Missouri was standing by the Union?"

"Split. Nobody knows for sure which way it will go."

Miller grunted. "I'm betting they'll stick with us. Figure this here Territory'll do the same, don't you?"

Jeff nodded. "Won't be easy. According to the report General Carleton got, Texas lined up with the South first thing."

Miller whistled softly. "What about all that army we had over there?"

"Twigg surrendered the whole works to the Confederacy—a million dollars worth of equipment and supplies."

The sergeant mopped at sweat with a horny hand, wagged his head. "Ain't no sense to it—us fighting amongst ourselves."

"Davis figures he's right, same as President Lincoln thinks he is. We can't let the country break into two pieces."

"Well, I sure hate missing all the fireworks," Miller drawled. "Half a mind to ask the General for—"

First Sergeant Amos Miller began to die in that next moment, an arrow piercing his throat. Marshak heard a strange gasping sound come from his lips, turned to look.

The old noncom, a surprised frown on his beaten features, was sliding forward, settling on the floor of the wagon.

Gunshots rang out in that succeeding instant and the sweltering hush erupted with yells. Marshak seized the reins from Miller's convulsing hand and glanced at the escort wheeling uncertainly in a boiling cloud of dust.

Rising to his feet like a Roman chariot driver, he whipped the mules into a gallop. From the tail of his eye he saw Harry Wills fall from the saddle. Kennerman, revolver blasting, was cutting in close, planning to take a position close to the wagon.

Bucknell was down. Jeff saw Rudd pull his horse to an abrupt halt, three arrows stiff and horizontal in his back. The man was dead but didn't know it. An Apache wheeled in through the confusion, skewered the cavalryman with his lance, sent him spilling to the ground. Marshak couldn't locate Conroy or Krause, guessed they, too, were dead.

He was alone. Ambrose Kennerman's riderless horse pounded alongside, keeping pace with the mules, and then it swung away as the Apaches pressed in. Grim, Jeff dropped back onto the seat and braced himself. Resting his rifle upon the forearm of the hand that held the reins, he began to make use of it.

2

Marshak, blood and sweat stinging his eyes, whirled onto Whiterock's parade ground, slowed the lathered team to a trot and finally halted them before a thin crowd of officers and enlisted men gathered in front of what apparently served as general headquarters. The place was more a camp than a fort, he noted, it being simply a collection of temporary buildings and canvas tents with no surrounding wall or stockade fence.

Two privates stepped up, caught the dust-plastered mules by the bridles. An officer wearing the gold leaves of a major pushed forward, walking stiffly erect as he cut a passage through the gathering.

"Who are you, mister, and where are you from?" he asked with no preliminaries.

The major was a graying, iron-jawed man with cold eyes. Marshak stared at him silently for a long moment, disengaged his feet from Miller's body and dropped to the ground.

"Captain Jeff Marshak. Second California Cavalry. On special assignment, sir," he said, saluting wearily.

"Major Jeremiah Denton, post commander in the absence of Colonel Ronald Searcy," the older man stated. "How many men did you lose?"

"Seven."

Denton frowned. "Fool stunt—trying to cross this country with seven men. Whose stupid idea was this, Captain?"

A woman emerged from headquarters—a girl, to be more exact. She was dark, had wide-spaced eyes and full lips that were parted in a slight smile. Denton's wife, Marshak guessed, then reckoned she'd more likely be his daughter; she bore herself in that same supercilious manner.

"Mine," he said, brushing tiredly at his chin. "Idea was to attract as little attention as possible."

Denton sniffed. "Well, no matter now. I'll expect you in my office with a full report as soon as you're in condition to do so. Post surgeon will see to your wounds."

Jeff inclined his head slightly, saluted again. Denton pivoted, strode toward his quarters. A ruddy-faced young second lieutenant stepped up, made his recognition.

"Lieutenant Francis Kime, sir. I'll see your animals are cared for."

"Be obliged," Marshak said. "Tell the detail to leave the wagon be—not touch it."

Kime looked bewildered, paused. "But the dead man—"

"I'm talking about the cargo. Have Sergeant Miller removed, of course."

"Yes, sir," Kime said, color rising in his neck. "I'll see to it."

Marshak grinned, breaking the gullied lines of his face. He had little fear of anyone discovering the War Chest while pawing about in the wagon's contents; it was safely hidden beneath a false floor in the vehicle. Nevertheless, he would just as soon that nobody made any close inspection.

"Captain—"

Jeff turned wearily, found the girl standing before him. He

touched the brim of his hat and she smiled, exposing twin rows of even, white teeth.

"I'm Marcie Denton. I'll take you to the surgeon, if you wish."

Marshak nodded, said, "Kind of you."

He fell in beside her, halted. The detail that had driven off the Apaches was filing back onto the parade. One man lay across the saddle of his horse. Jeff glanced at the officer in the lead, a stiff-shouldered lieutenant with the suggestion of a beard taking shape on his face.

"Carey Mossman," Marcie volunteered. "He won't like losing a man, even if it meant saving your skin."

"We don't choose our fate," Marshak murmured, irritated, and glanced at Mossman. "Survivors?"

The officer's features were grim. "None. Savages had stripped and butchered them. I buried them where they lay."

Marshak looked down. "I'll make up the family notifications."

Mossman's tone was hard. "What in the name of God were you doing out there with only a handful of men? Any fool ought to know—"

"We all go by orders," Marshak said curtly, and wheeled away.

Immediately Marcie hurried to overtake him. She laughed, the sound of it ragging his jaded nerves.

"Told you Carey wouldn't appreciate it. Proud of the fact he's never lost a man under his command—up till now, that is."

"How long's he been pulling duty here?"

"About a year, I think. Been here only a couple of months myself—visiting my father."

"He'll learn," Marshak said dryly. "Spit and polish boys from the Point all do—if they live long enough."

He glanced up, watched Mossman and his troopers crossing the sun-baked ground, heading for a small building at the upper end of the parade.

"That the extent of your cavalry?"

Marcie nodded. "Just about. This is an infantry post."

Infantry! What the hell good was infantry out here, Marshak wondered.

"Here's the surgery," Marcie said, turning into a walk that led to another of the same characterless structures making up the post. Opening the screened door, she stepped inside.

Jeff followed her into the breathless depths of a large room rank with the odors of carbolic acid and other medicines. An officer, devoid of coat and with his shirt collar open at the neck in deference to the heat, arose from a desk in a far corner.

"Major Lockwood, Captain Marshak," Marcie said. "Captain needs a little attention."

Jeff slid a glance at the girl, irritation again rising within him. She had an edged way of saying things, giving them an ironic tinge. He wasn't sure he could take much of Marcie Denton without losing his temper.

"So I see," the surgeon murmured, coming nearer. "That you all the hullabaloo was about?"

Marshak shrugged. "Apaches jumped us. I was the lucky one."

"But not so lucky you didn't get a few nicks."

"A few."

"Let's get that shirt off," Lockwood said, all business. He hesitated, cocked his head at Marcie. "Young lady, I think you—"

She giggled. "Don't mind me, Major. I've seen men without shirts before." Crossing the room, she perched herself on a corner of a desk.

Lockwood tossed Marshak's bloodstained garment onto a chair, pointed to a metal examining table near the window. "Climb up," he directed, and reached for a basin of water. Soaking a cloth, he scrubbed gently at Jeff's neck and arm.

"Where from, Mr. Marshak?"

"California," Marcie answered promptly before Jeff could speak. "On special assignment of some sort. His whole escort was wiped out. Carey Mossman lost a man rescuing him. What sort of special duty, Captain?"

"One I don't talk about," Marshak said coolly.

Lockwood laughed, cast a sidelong look at the girl as he opened a glass case filled with bottles and rolls of cotton and bandages.

"Guess that'll hold you, missy," he said, obviously enjoying the rebuff handed her. "Now, why don't you get out of here and leave the Captain to me?"

"Because I'm waiting for him, that's why. He's the first person to arrive at this post in more than a month—since the trouble started, in fact." After a moment she added petulantly, "Nobody ever comes to Whiterock anymore."

"We may get more visitors than we've bargained for," the surgeon said quietly.

Marshak winced as Lockwood probed the tear in his arm, then looked closely at the older officer.

"That remark have something to do with the war?"

The surgeon stared at him briefly, then shook his head. "Of course! Being on the road, you wouldn't have heard. Has to do with the war, all right."

Marshak fell silent as dull worry crept into his mind. "Be specific, Major. What's happened? Important to me."

Lockwood began to wind a bandage around the injured arm. "Baylor's moved north—from Fort Bliss. He's occupied Mesilla with a fair-sized army of Rebels."

So the war had come to New Mexico. Jeff considered that. Then: "What about Fort Fillmore?"

"Lynde abandoned the place, tried to make it to Fort Craig. Baylor caught him. Reports are now that the Confederates will march north, take Craig, Santa Fe and go on to Fort Union."

"Goddammit!" Marshak exploded, forgetting the girl's presence. "Where's the Army?"

"No troops available. Canby petitioned for men, got no response. Need every available soldier elsewhere, I suppose. We heard they were preparing for a big ruckus somewhere in Virginia. . . . There, that ought to hold your arm. Now I'll have a look at that lump on your head."

"This mean you'll have to stay on at the post for a while?" Marcie asked, moving to the window.

Jeff shifted his eyes to her. She was framed by the opening, face turned from him as she looked out over the cactus- and yucca-studded miles of gleaming, heat-tortured land to the rear of the fort. Little more than personal pleasure and selfish interest would occupy her mind.

"No," he said flatly, again wincing as Lockwood daubed disinfectant into his scalp. "Moving on soon as I can arrange for another escort."

The surgeon paused. "You're asking Denton—uh—the Major for men?"

"No other choice."

Lockwood resumed his task. "Suggest you wait until the Colonel returns. Think you'll find him a bit more receptive to your request."

"When's he due?"

"That I can't say. Could be today—or a week."

Jeff Marshak slid off the table. *Make all haste,* his orders read. *Permit no unseemly delay. The immediate completion of your mission is of vital importance. It may well have great bearing on the fate of the Union.* The high-flown words trickled through his memory. Boiled down, it amounted to one thing: Get to Washington with the cargo in the shortest time possible.

And to assist him in accomplishing this, he had the necessary authority strapped in a leather pouch hung around his waist—authority he was to use, however, only as a last resort. The fewer who knew of the importance of his mission, the better. Those were the Secretary's own words.

"Can't wait," he said, reaching for his tattered, stained shirt.

Lockwood checked him. "Here, probably got a clean one that'll fit," he said, and stepped to a closet beyond the desk. Selecting a carelessly folded shirt from other items on a shelf, he tossed it to Jeff. "Still think you'd be smart to wait for the Colonel."

Marshak pulled on the garment, settled it about his shoulders. "No time, Major. . . . Obliged to you for the shirt and the treatment."

The surgeon bobbed his head. "What I'm here for. Luck," he said and turned to his cabinet of medicines.

Jeff felt Marcie's arm slide in under his. "Now, I expect you'd better hurry over and see my father. He'll be waiting for your report."

A bath and some rest would be more to Jeff Marshak's liking, but Denton had impressed him as being a difficult man, one exalted by the authority temporarily resting upon his shoulders. Best he cater to the officer's ego.

"What I had in mind," he said, and followed her into the open.

3

Fort Whiterock lay silent in the broiling sun and there was little evidence of life as Marshak, nostrils curling at the smell of his own sweaty body, followed Marcie Denton back along the hard pack to headquarters where the post CO maintained his office.

Mounting the two steps to the porch, they crossed, entered. An aging sergeant at a desk in the rear center of the stuffy room glanced up, half rose to make a negligent salute.

"Major's waiting inside—sir," he said and jerked his head at an open door to the left.

Marcie, ignoring procedure, had not paused, simply marched by the noncom into a hall off which two other rooms lay, and led him to a third at the extreme rear. Marshak stepped into the confines of trapped heat, halted before Denton sitting rigid in a battered swivel chair. At closer quarters he had a better look at the officer. The major was an austere, humorless man and bitterness rode him like a brooding eagle. It was difficult to imagine that anyone, not even his wife, would have ever dared address him as anything other than Jeremiah.

Off to the left, near a window, First Lieutenant Carey Mossman leaned against the wall. Jeff saw the younger man's face color slightly and a stiffness come over him when he saw Marcie. Jealous, Jeff thought. The poor fool. Marcie would lead him a miserable life. He cut his attention back to Denton, saluted.

"All right, Captain," the senior officer said testily. "Let's have it—short and sweet."

Marshak made his report of the incident in half a dozen equally terse sentences. When he had finished, Denton scowled, pursed his lips.

"Twenty-five Apaches, you say? Mr. Mossman reports no more than half that number."

"Mr. Mossman wasn't there when it started," Jeff said brusquely. "My men accounted for—"

"To be sure," Denton said with a wave of his hand. "You think they were Cochise's people or Pinals?"

"Haven't the faintest idea," Marshak said. "First time I've encountered Apaches."

"Not your last, I'm sure. They're up in arms, raising hob throughout the country."

Jeff frowned. He had a long journey ahead of him and the thought of continual brushes with hostile Indians wasn't particularly comforting.

"My understanding of the situation in the Territory was that we were at peace with the tribes."

"Your understanding is a bit outdated. We were getting along with them until Bascom lost his head."

"Bascom?"

"Lieutenant Bascom. Had a run-in with Cochise last April. Hung some of the chief's relatives, started Cochise on a blood trail that'll be hard to stop. . . . Can't say as I blame Bascom much, though. Likely done the same had I been in his boots."

Marshak shifted heavily. A local problem, but one that could mean trouble for him. However, there was little he could do about it. He glanced meaningfully at Mossman and Marcie Denton, wishing they would leave. He could do without the audience.

"Your orders, mister."

Jeff came up sharply at the officer's stiffly-put request. Reaching inside his waistband, he unhooked the flat leather pouch, released its twin buckles and selected a letter from among other papers. Silent, he handed it to Denton who unfolded the sheet slowly.

"Thomas Jefferson Marshak," he read aloud, lips curling slightly, and then fell silent as he perused the balance of the writing. Finished, he refolded the letter, returned it to Jeff.

"Signed by Carleton," he said. "Just what is the nature of this duty to which you're assigned, Captain?"

Again Marshak touched the girl and Carey Mossman with his eyes. "Not a matter for general conversation, sir."

Denton cleared his throat impatiently. "Oh, come now, Mr. Marshak. It's Army business, isn't it? I daresay anything you tell me will not fall upon unfriendly ears. Lieutenant Mossman is as much a part of the Army as you, and my daughter, well—"

"I prefer not to discuss it openly."

"You prefer!" Denton exploded suddenly. "Just who do you think you are, mister? I'll remind you that I'm in charge of this post and, as such, your commanding officer!"

"I'm aware of that," Marshak replied quietly. "No disrespect intended." He'd antagonized the officer despite his determination to do otherwise; Jeremiah Denton, however, had an extremely short fuse. "Fact is I'm directed to use extreme care."

"Indeed. . . . Hardly applicable here, Captain. Let's have the details."

Anger had begun to simmer within Jeff Marshak. What the hell was wrong with Denton? Couldn't he get it through his thick head that it was confidential?

"I repeat—I'm not at liberty to reveal the nature of my mission," he said coolly. Opening his pouch, he returned Carleton's letter to its place, faced Denton. "I assume my report was acceptable—and my orders. I'd like to place a request with you, sir."

A stillness settled over the officer's features. "Request?"

Marcie Denton smiled brightly at her father. "He wants an escort—one to replace—"

"What's this?" Denton shouted, coming up straight in his chair.

Marshak gave the girl an exasperated look, nodded. "It's necessary that I continue without delay. I need seven men—six cavalrymen and a teamster."

"Seven men!" the officer echoed, his voice thick with sarcasm. "Just like that—seven men!" He leaned forward. "Are you out of your mind? I couldn't spare one, not one!"

"Afraid you'll have to, Major," Jeff said. He had hoped it wouldn't be necessary to produce the letter of authority he carried—the one from Washington—but it appeared he had no alternative.

Denton, fuming silently, leaned on his elbows. Sweat clung to his brows, made small, shining patches on his cheeks. "That sounds like a threat, mister."

Marshak, weary of fencing, shrugged. "No threat, just a statement of fact. Be glad to go further into it if we can do so in private."

Mossman, wholly quiet during the interview, stepped forward. Dust still covered his clothing and he, too, was perspiring profusely.

"If you're finished with me, sir," he said hesitantly, making his salute.

Denton chewed at his lower lip momentarily, debating the advisability of keeping the officer present in disregard of Marshak's insistence, decided against it. He made a motion with his hand.

"Dismissed, Lieutenant. . . . Dismissed."

Mossman spun on his heel, glanced at Marcie, and then stalked down the hallway to disappear into the outer office. Marshak swung his eyes to the girl. She smiled sweetly.

"All right, Daughter," Denton said in a tone that said he was simply humoring Marshak. "Seems the Captain has a dark secret not for your ears."

Marcie flipped her head, smiled again, but there was conscious effort in it this time. "Of course, Papa," she said and marched across the room. Reaching the doorway, she halted, turned, mood again changing. "The Captain will, of course, have dinner with us this evening."

"He will, he will," Denton said impatiently.

Marcie bobbed her head at Jeff. "I'll see you later then," she said and moved on.

Marshak stepped to the inner door, pushed it shut, thus closing off the sergeant in the adjoining room, came back to Denton.

"I'll place my request with you formally, Major; six cavalrymen and a teamster—to leave first thing in the morning."

"And I'll tell you again, Captain, I won't comply," the officer said, rising and seeking the cooler clime near the window. "I can't—and it's about time others learned this is no replacement center for every—"

"Before you say more," Jeff cut in, reaching into the pouch again, "I suggest you read this letter."

Denton, watching through narrowed eyes, accepted the envelope. "Occurs to me, I could bring you up before a court-martial for your attitude, Mr. Marshak," he said in a low voice. "Nobody can come into—"

"The letter—sir. I suggest you look at it."

Denton glared, but he opened the envelope, unfolded the sheet of crisp paper and began to read. His expression altered visibly. Finished, he read it a second time, finally returned it to its container.

"Chase, eh," he murmured. "And countersigned by General Scott." Irritable, he handed the envelope back to Jeff. "Damned easy for them to sit there on their behinds in Washington and write directives like that. Don't have the vaguest notion what we're up against here in the sticks."

"Perhaps," Marshak said, putting the letter away. "Fact remains that I'm to be given priority in any and all matters pertaining to the immediate completion of my mission. I assume you are now agreeable to my request."

"Seems I have no choice," Denton said stiffly. "But you'll wait."

"Wait? Time is something I can't spare, Major. The letter makes that clear."

"The hell with your letter! I can only do so much, being shorthanded as it is. This is an infantry post, Captain; we have only a small detachment of cavalry. I can do nothing for you until Lieutenant Jackman returns."

"When do you expect him?"

"Today, probably."

"There's a chance then I can pull out of here in the morning."

"Very possibly. No guarantee."

Jeff sighed wearily. "Guess that will have to do."

"Appears now you don't have any choice, regardless of Chase's letter," Denton said, a note of triumph in his tone.

Crossing to his desk, he opened a drawer, drew forth a box of cigars. Helping himself, he started to replace the weeds, and then having an afterthought, pushed the box at Marshak. Jeff shook his head.

"Tell me, Captain," the officer said, closing the drawer, "what's in that wagon you're so anxious to deliver? Must be mighty important to rate a letter from the Secretary of the Treasury and General Scott both."

Jeff shook his head. "Don't ask me that, sir. I'm under orders not to discuss it with anyone."

Denton bit off the end of his cigar, spat it aside and fished inside his pocket for a match. "Surely doesn't include an officer of higher rank—"

"It does—regardless of rank."

Anger flickered in the post commander's small eyes. "Oh, very well—forget it," he said, striking his match and inhaling deeply. Blowing a cloud of smoke into the stale, heat-laden air, he cocked his head to one side and regarded Jeff slyly. "However, it doesn't take much imagination to figure it out.

"A letter from high places passing you through with top priority. A cargo from California—where all the gold comes from. . . . Gold—that's what your cargo consists of, isn't it, Captain?"

The man was a fool, a damned fool, Jeff thought. He should know better than to pry. Disgusted, Marshak took a half-step back, brought his arm to a stiff salute.

"I believe we have no further business to transact, Major. With your permission—"

Denton laughed, clearly pleased with himself. "Sure, sure—dismissed," he said. "I'll expect you for supper. . . . We dine at five. . . . Meanwhile, bunk in at bachelor officers quarters. I'll have Sergeant Mayfield conduct you—"

"No need," Marshak said. "I'll find it."

Marcie stood at the window in the parlor of their makeshift house—everything in Whiterock was makeshift—and waited. When she saw Jeff Marshak, tall and rack-shouldered, emerge from headquarters building, she felt again a strong stir of interest. Moving nearer, she pulled the flowered chintz curtain aside for a better look.

His somewhat square face with its overshot brow was set to hard lines and the man's strength of purpose was like a flat sheen pushing through dark, wind-burned skin. She wondered how he'd make out with his request; her father would have fought granting it—that was certain. And Marshak—what nationality was he anyway?—would have been equally insistent. Somehow she had the feeling that he'd won out.

She watched him tread the short walk to the street, pause, swing his glance around in a slow circle as if making his bitter assessment of the fort, and then move on. Down to his left where the unmarried officers quartered she saw Carey Mossman appear at the door wearing only breeches and undershirt, hair ruffled and going in all directions. Evidently he had just completed his bath, was preparing himself for the coming evening.

Carey didn't like Marshak, that was plain. And it wouldn't help matters any when he learned the Californian would be dining with the Dentons while he was being pointedly ignored. He'd be furious. . . . That was a delicious thought—but Carey Mossman was taking too much for granted. The jolt would do him good.

Marshak swung down the street, pointing for the stables at the far end of the parade. She liked the way he walked, easy and sure, the stride of a healthy man knowing exactly where he was going—and why. Again something stirred within her, aroused by the sheer masculinity of the man.

He halted at the wagon he had brought in, disappeared briefly under its canvas arch to reappear with a fresh uniform draped over his arm. Private Agnew came from the stable at that moment and the two men conversed for a short time. Then, following Agnew's leveled finger, Marshak headed for BOQ.

Carey, she noted, no longer stood in the doorway when the Californian reached the low, rambling building, and entered. Marcie remained at the window wondering what would be passing between them, and then remembering her purpose, turned and walked to the kitchen.

Mattie, the combination housekeeper and cook, looked up through wisps of stringy gray hair that partially blocked her vision.

"We'll have a guest for supper," Marcie said, glancing to the sideboard where preparations for the meal were already underway. She made a wry face. Steak again. . . . The usual side dishes of greens, rice and potatoes. She'd hoped for something different for a change.

"No need telling me," Mattie said, wiping sweat from her face with a corner of her apron. "That Lieutenant Mossman's been eating here every night since you come."

"I don't mean him."

The elderly woman paused. "It ain't the Lieutenant?"

"No—Captain Marshak. He's the one who just arrived. From California."

Mattie nodded slowly. "So now it's another'n, eh? Why ain't you having the Lieutenant, too?"

"Because I don't want to!" Marcie snapped.

"Reckon you know what you're doing," Mattie said, now shaking her head, "but if you was to ask me I'd say you was making a mistake. Way I hear it this here Captain ain't staying around for long."

There's nothing faster than an Army post grapevine, Marcie thought. "Well, I'm not asking you. I know exactly what I'm doing. Carey Mossman has no claim on me—and it's high time he realized it."

"Maybe—"

"Maybe—fiddlesticks! What are we having for dessert?"

"Bread puddin', same as—"

"Oh, Mattie—no! An apple pie, that's what we should have. Men all love apple pie."

The cook mopped at her face again, continued her potato peeling. "You want apple pie, you make it. Apples're there in the cupboard."

"And get all red from the stove's heat? It would spoil my face. Please, Mattie, you do it."

The older woman wagged her head. "Won't have no time."

"It's early—you'll have plenty of time." Marcie paused, smiled sweetly. "Maybe if you'd take a small drink from that bottle you've got hidden in the broom closet—that Father doesn't know about—you'd find time."

Mattie laid down her paring knife, folded her hands. "You been spying on me?" she demanded accusingly.

"No, just came across it accidently. I'm supposed to oversee everything here in the house, you know, report anything that's not right."

Mattie stared at the girl for a long moment, and then her shoulders went down. "We'll have apple pie," she mumbled.

4

"That," Jeff Marshak said, rising and drawing back Marcie Denton's chair, "was the finest meal I've had in years. Apple pie was particularly good."

The girl laughed gaily. "Oh, our Mattie's a jewel," she said and glanced toward the kitchen door where she knew the old cook would be eavesdropping. "Father says her cooking is the only thing that makes life bearable in this God-forsaken wilderness—to use his own words."

Across the table Jeremiah Denton nodded confirmation as he also got to his feet. Within the confines of his home his attitude had softened slightly.

"Exactly the way I feel," he declared. "Bad enough to be relegated to a post such as this—two thousand miles from civilization—without being plagued with dyspepsia. . . . Suggest we retire to the verandah. A trifle cooler there, perhaps."

Marcie placed her hands together. "That's a good idea, Papa! I'll ask Mattie to make lemonade. You go ahead—I'll join you shortly."

Major Denton looked more directly at his daughter as if wondering why the custom they followed each evening should evoke such unprecedented delight, but having better than average understanding of his daughter, he said nothing, simply turned and led the way to the porch.

The two men settled down in wicker chairs, Denton with his cigar, Marshak, beginning to feel the weight of the day, with his thoughts. He had lost seven men—seven good men; and despite a long-past resolution never to permit himself to get close to subordinates, the matter lay heavily upon his mind. . . . Miller. . . . Rudd. . . . Ambrose Kennerman—the new man, Krause. . . . Conroy—

"Pleasant evening." Denton's comment made him aware of the moment.

"Indeed," Jeff replied. "Any word from Jackman?"

Denton sucked thoughtfully on his cigar, shook his head. "None. Disturbs me somewhat."

Across the way Carey Mossman and young Francis Kime stepped from the mess hall, paused on the steps. Kime was speaking animatedly, now and then emphasizing a point by pounding an open palm with a knotted fist. Mossman appeared to be only half listening, his attention instead on Denton and Marshak taking their ease on the verandah.

At that moment Marcie came from the interior of the house. She had changed into a soft-blue full skirt and a daintily edged shirtwaist of snowy white, cut low at the neck. She was carrying a tray upon which were three glasses and a pitcher filled to the brim. Both men rose at once, Denton drawing up a small table for her convenience while Jeff dragged in a third chair, held it for her.

When the glasses were filled and all had sat, Denton gave her a bland glance. "You've changed."

Marcie smiled prettily, fingered the lace of her collar. "I thought this would be cooler."

"Unquestionably," the officer said dryly.

She turned to Jeff. "And does it have your approval, Captain?"

Mossman and Kime had moved on, clean, sharp figures in the slanting sunlight. He swung his attention to the girl. "Very fetching."

Marcie sniffed. "Is that the best you can do?"

He smiled, relieving the hard, tired lines of his face. "I could say you make a most attractive and pretty picture—and mean every word of it."

"That's much better," Marcie said with an exaggerated show of satisfaction. She took up the pitcher, leaned toward him. "Have more, Captain. I'm sorry there's no ice, but the water is cool."

He thanked her, murmured, "It is delicious."

Denton harrumphed, studied the tip of his cigar. "Thinking about this mission you're on. Still believe it was foolhardy to undertake it with so small an escort, considering your—ah—cargo. Would appear to me a full company would be more in order."

Jeff had hoped the post's commander would avoid the subject but, rankling him, it seemed it was yet caught in his throat.

"A large force would have drawn attention," he said.

"Not exactly clear thinking."

"You were having no Indian trouble when I started," Jeff reminded the officer. "Thus danger from that point was thought to be negligible."

"Just what is this mysterious mission you're on?" Marcie demanded impatiently. "You both act so strange and secretive!"

Denton chuckled. "The Captain doesn't talk of it. He has a flair, I fear, for the—the mysterious, as you put it."

Marshak ignored the veiled jibe, stared out over the parade. Shadows were beginning to lengthen, and where the enlisted men lived in their tents and crude shacks, the first signs of activity were becoming evident. The vulnerability of Fort Whiterock bothered Jeff Marshak; it was like no encampment he'd ever seen.

"Apaches been quite troublesome in this area?" he asked.

"Always troublesome," Denton said. "Just more so since the Bascom affair. Not safe for a man to move about after dark—even here inside the fort. Occasions when savages have actually prowled the area."

"Inside the fort?" Jeff repeated, astonished.

Denton nodded. "Rule here is, Captain—if you take a stroll, keep your sidearm handy."

It was unbelievable—but understandable. "Why hasn't a wall or a stockade fence been erected? You need the protection it would afford."

"Agreed—and it's a good question. But we're the stepchild of official Washington. We're begrudingly allotted only the necessities—and someone back there apparently doesn't feel such measures are necessary. We're tabbed as a temporary camp but have all the responsibilities of a fort—"

"Now, Papa," Marcie broke in hurriedly, "you'll get yourself all worked up—and it's much too hot—"

"The devil with the heat! I'll say it to Marshak and maybe he'll repeat it where it'll do some good! A lot of things we need, Captain—more men, more horses, more equipment—money to do something with!"

Denton hurled his cigar into the yard, raised himself higher in his chair. "You think I wouldn't like to see a wall or at least a six-foot fence around this place? You think requisitions for them haven't been made, time after time? Dozens of them—and what has it accomplished? Absolutely nothing. We're supposed to just squat here and bake—roast, and hope the Apaches or the Pinals don't someday take it on themselves to overrun us."

"A likely possibility," Marshak murmured. "Any timber around close? Men could put in their idle time cutting and hauling in posts for a stockade."

The older officer motioned toward the distant mountains.

"Timber there, of course, but getting it takes official approval—and we can't get it. Whiterock was established as a temporary camp. Purpose—give aid to travelers making the trip across country to California, and vice versa. We've been here longer now than originally intended. Thus we're permitted nothing. In effect, our orders are simply to remain status quo—exist until someone in Washington decides we can consolidate with Fort Buchanan or Breckenridge, or some other establishment."

Marshak shook his head slowly. "I think," he said, "I'd proceed with fortifications, approval or not. With the war very possibly shifting this direction—"

"The war, Captain? It'll be over and done with before we get the first dispatches from Washington. What fighting's to be done will take place in Virginia or the Carolinas. Mark my words—it'll create not one ripple west of the Mississippi."

"They take a dimmer view of it back in the Capitol."

"Desk soldiers!" Denton snorted. "What else could you expect? Lacking any actual experience—and with a nonmilitary man at the head of the government—"

The officer broke off, muttering to himself. Marshak remained silent, continued to study the deserted parade where dust particles hung in spinning suspension in the slanting beams of sunlight. Carey Mossman and Kime appeared in the wide doorway of the stable, halted. At once Marcie rose to her feet, leaned against the porch railing and smiled down at Jeff.

"It's not half so bad as my father would have you believe. Really, it isn't."

"It's a hell of a life," the officer countered grumpily. "Man wastes himself away, accomplishes absolutely nothing. All those years spent in service—and for what? For this. . . . There's no justice in the Army anymore—no fairness. You'll agree to that, Captain?"

Marshak placed his empty glass on the table. "Army means a lot to me. And I've learned a man takes what's handed him if he wants peace with himself. I've been satisfied, perhaps not always happy."

"Where you from? Always California?"

"Originally New York. Transferred to General Carleton's command in fifty-seven."

"Know the general only vaguely. What sort of—"

"Can't you men talk of anything but the Army?" Marcie exclaimed impatiently, a half smile parting her lips. "I refuse to sit here and be ignored any longer!"

Jeff grinned, sat up in his chair. "My apologies—"

Denton bobbed his head. "Of course, of course. We both apologize. Only that I don't often get the chance to talk shop with an outsider."

"Well, you've talked it enough for one day—I'm taking charge now," the girl said firmly. "Tomorrow you can air your views all you wish. The Captain and I are going on a tour of the post."

Denton squinted at Jeff. "The Captain's had a hard day," he said reprovingly. "Expect he'd enjoy a night's rest more than a tour."

"That didn't stop you from talking—"

"I'd enjoy a stroll," Marshak broke in, getting to his feet. "Fact is, I'd planned to look in on my mules."

"Then go, by all means," the major said. "I've a bit of reading to do myself." He shifted his eyes to Marcie, shook a warning finger at her. "Remember the rules, girl. I want you safely inside this house by full dark."

"Oh, I'll be in good care," Marcie said lightly, taking Jeff's arm and drawing him toward the steps. "Don't worry."

The post commander rose. "Of course—but you'll see that you're back here on time, nevertheless."

"Of course," she said, mimicking him, and moved out onto the walk with Marshak.

Five miles east of Whiterock, in a narrow, rock-faced defile through which the road to Fort Craig cuts its path, Ross Conroy stirred restlessly and fingered the bloodstained scarf wrapped around his arm. He was cold and the wound he'd received during the brush with the Apaches pained him.

"You sure he'll be coming this way?"

"How many times I going to have to tell you so?" Wade Krause demanded in his dry, raspy way. "Said I'd seen that map he's following. Goes right from Whiterock to Craig."

"Maybe he'll change—"

"Now why in the hell would he do that? Only one road to Craig. He's got to go by it." Krause paused, spat angrily. "Goddamnit, cut out your worrying about it!"

"Reckon I can't help it."

Krause groaned, wagged his head. "Sure wish it was Rudd here, instead of you partnering up with me. Had this whole thing worked out between us—then them damned 'Paches had to mess it up."

Conroy plucked at his bandage. "It's just that I ain't so certain it'll be all that easy, like you claim."

"Why won't it? Couldn't find no better spot for an ambush. And picking off the escort'll be a cinch—like dippin' whiskey out of a washtub."

"They'll be using carbines, too."

"Don't mean nothing. Holed up here in these rocks, we can shoot them out of the saddle before they know what's hit 'em."

Conroy was quiet for a time, listening to the distant barking of a coyote. "Waiting's making me jumpy."

"You sound like some green kid. Hell, you been on night patrol before."

"Wasn't nothing like this. How much gold did you say was in that wagon?"

"Couple hundred thousand dollars worth—maybe even more. Never did hear for sure, but it'll be a god's plenty. Keep us living high on the hog rest of our lives."

"Hope so. Ain't got no craving for being stood up against a wall and shot for a deserter—"

"Aw, for hell's sake, you're talking like we was going to get caught. It's less'n a day to the border. Once we cross over there ain't nobody can touch us."

"Still got to get there."

Krause stirred, swore helplessly. "Jeez!" he muttered. "Why'd it have to be old Rudd? Why couldn't it have been you them stinking 'Paches got instead of him?"

5

With Marcie Denton clinging to his arm, Marshak turned into the street. Across the way a guard detail was marching out to take up posts along the perimeter of the fort, and seeing that, he felt better. At least some precautions were taken.

Lamps were coming on in the huts and tents making up the compound, and somewhere beyond the half-wood, half-canvas quartermaster's building a man with a tenor voice was singing softly to the accompaniment of a mouth harp. It was that pleasant time of day, that hazy interlude between last golden light and full dark when a hush falls over the land and all sounds seem distant and bell-clear.

The hour never failed to move Jeff Marshak, stir within him the buried skeins of loneliness, remind him of the things he'd missed and other men possessed. But he was one slow to regret; he'd lived his life each day as it had been presented to him by whatever powers control, and he was satisfied. To him the act of living, seasoned with duty, was in itself a privilege.

"Have you always been Army, Captain?"

The sound of Marcie's voice lifted him from the well of thought. He nodded.

"All my life, practically."

"You're not from the Academy."

He laughed. "You were the one who said we weren't to talk shop. Matter of record, no. Does it show?"

"Well—it's easy to tell."

"Easy? How?"

"You're less formal, for one thing—not so stiff and correct all the time. Maybe," she frowned, pursed her lips, "it's the way you walk, carry yourself—so straight yet not so unbending, if you know what I mean."

He laughed again. "Afraid not."

"And you're sort of sure of yourself, like you didn't owe allegiance to anyone, only to yourself, and what you think is right."

"Is that bad?"

"I guess not. But it doesn't leave much room for anything else, does it?"

Marshak gave the girl an oblique look. "If you mean for a home—a family, I suppose not."

"Don't you ever intend to marry?"

He shrugged, uncomfortable with the topic. "It's possible—someday."

"Someday!" she exclaimed, waving her hands. "When that someday comes you could be too old!"

"Doubt if age has much to do with love," he said. "Right now I'm where I want to be—in the Army doing what I like best—"

"A soldier."

"A soldier, and with war breaking out—"

"For God and Country!" she quoted airily.

"For that and whatever else," he said quietly.

They had reached the extreme southern end of the street, crossed over and were beginning to double back, walking slowly through the clashing odors of fried food, dust and desert sage. Carey Mossman, alone now, stood framed in the doorway of BOQ, features stilled as he followed them with his eyes. Jeff glanced at Marcie. She was ignoring the officer, with an expression of smugness on her lovely face.

Chagrin stiffened him. He'd just then realized it, but he was being used—and used good. Marcie was flaunting him before the lieutenant.

"Think I'll follow the Major's suggestion, get myself some sleep," he said.

She drew back in dismay. "So early? We haven't even made the circle! You disappoint me, Captain."

He moved his shoulders wearily. "All right, the circle. I'll have a look at my team—and then it's good night."

Marcie smiled, threw a furtive look toward Mossman. She gripped Jeff's arm tighter. "My father tells me you're to get your escort. How in the world did you persuade him?"

"He didn't tell you?"

"Only that you're on some sort of secret mission, one of importance." She hesitated, smiled ruefully. "I tried to wheedle it out of him, but failed."

Marshak's estimation of Jeremiah Denton climbed a notch.

"What is the mission, Captain?"

He shook his head, refusing to answer.

"Must be terribly important—you're so grim and close-mouthed about it. And Father—usually I can find out anything I want from him."

"Appreciate his not going into it," Jeff said. "What do you do around here to pass the time since it's dangerous to leave the fort?"

"There's absolutely nothing to do," she declared, pouting prettily. "Just nothing! I get so tired of it. There are no girls my age I can associate with—and we never go to Tubac anymore."

Tubac. . . . He recalled his map. A fair-sized settlement to the south. "Aren't there any young wives on the base—officer's wives, I mean?"

"All the junior officers are bachelors."

"Not all—for long."

She halted, faced him. "Just what does that mean?"

"Lieutenant Mossman. Don't tell me he hasn't asked you to marry him."

Her eyes widened in surprise, and then she caught herself. "Carey? Oh, many times—but it's all his idea."

"You certain of that?"

"Of course!" she said sharply.

"Then why go to all this trouble of making him jealous? I'm not blind."

"Jealous! You think he means anything to me—so much I'd bother? I couldn't care less."

"Sure, sure," Jeff said, grinning. He halted. They were in front of the stable. "Wait here a minute, then I'll walk you home."

She only nodded and he moved away from her, entered the shadow-filled structure housing the horses and mules. There was no one around and he finally located his team in a double stall at the far end of the runway.

The mules had enjoyed a rubdown, were contentedly munching at grain in the manger before them. The rest would do them good; they'd be in excellent condition to resume the journey.

Marshak started to retrace his steps, paused to examine the scratch the Apache lance had laid on the rump of one. It was no more than that and the hostler had already applied salve to the shallow cut.

Jeff wheeled, came up solidly against Marcie who had followed him silently into the building.

"Sorry—" he said, stepping back hurriedly. "I didn't know you were there."

She smiled quietly, her face tilted to his, invitation on her lips. "I—I wanted to be alone—with you."

He stared at her while the lines around his mouth grew hard. "Alone so you can have something to rub Mossman's wounds with—that it?"

"I just thought—"

"You thought by coming in here with me, you'd really have something to throw in his face! That's exactly what you thought. No thanks, Miss Denton. You're not making me the goat in your—"

Abruptly she threw her arms around his neck, went on tiptoe and kissed him hungrily on the lips. He swore harshly, jerked away. She fell back a step, watching him intently.

"Get out of here!" he snarled. "Get away from me before you start something you'll be sorry for!"

She remained frozen before him for a long, pulsating moment, and then a small sound escaped her lips. Whirling, she started down the runway, tripped, fell sprawling.

Jeff, anger still flooding him, leaped forward to aid her. She scrambled to her feet, flung him off, and bursting into tears, raced for the doorway.

"Wait!" he called.

She reached the entrance to the stable, hair now loose and hanging about her shoulders, bits of straw and trash clinging to her clothing, and bolted into the open.

Mossman, waiting outside his quarters, saw her plunge into the street, turn and run stumbling for the Denton house.

"Marcie!" he yelled, hurrying to intercept.

Sobbing, she fled on by. The officer stared at her for a few moments, then wheeled, headed for the stable at a brisk run. He met Jeff Marshak coming out.

"You—you bastard!" he shouted and swung a long, looping right fist.

Marshak dodged the blow easily. "Now—wait a minute, mister—"

"Wait—hell!" Mossman snapped, flaming with anger. "Might have known this would happen. . . . Comes from trying to make an officer and a gentleman out of a goddamned bohunk!"

Jeff hit him hard and clean on the point of the chin. The officer lifted on his heels, fell stiffly to the loose dust. Somewhere across the parade a voice shouted for the sergeant of the guard, and coming from BOQ was young Francis Kime, pulling on his shirt as he ran.

And still farther down the street Jeremiah Denton appeared, advancing in rapid, outraged strides.

6

Kime, sucking for breath, halted beside Mossman. He stared wonderingly at the officer's slack features, then raised his eyes to Marshak.

"What—"

"Throw some water on him, Lieutenant," Jeff said.

Two privates trotted up from the direction of the quartermaster building, both grinning secretly. Kime, remembering rank, relayed the order to them. The men swung aside, disappeared into the stable. At that moment Denton, flanked by another officer and First Sergeant Mayfield, arrived.

The post commander, lips compressed to a thin, gray line, moustache bristling, glanced only briefly at Mossman and then placed his splintering gaze on Jeff.

"I'll have you before a court-martial for this, mister!"

The two men accompanying Denton squatted beside Mossman, raised him to a sitting position. More soldiers drifted in, along with a few women.

Marshak studied the graying major thoughtfully. He seemed to think bringing charges against a man was the answer to everything.

"I don't take what he called me from any man," he said, finally.

"The devil with that—I'm talking about my daughter—your treatment of her!"

Jeff frowned. "Your daughter?"

"I saw what happened, Captain!"

Marshak stiffened and a stillness came over him. Carey Mossman was on his feet, eyes slightly glazed, but he was coming around fast—without benefit of water.

"You have anything to say, state it now," Denton snapped.

"I've said it. The Lieutenant made a remark that I resented."

"I'm not interested in that!" the older officer insisted angrily. "I'm speaking of the insult to my daughter."

Marshak stirred impatiently. "Insult! There was no insult."

"Don't deny it," Mossman broke in, now fully recovered. "I saw you take her into the stable, saw you—"

"Gentlemen," the officer who had been at Denton's side laid a hand on Mossman's arm. "Perhaps it would be better to discuss this matter in private," he said, glancing meaningfully around at the steadily growing crowd.

Jeremiah Denton seemingly became aware of the moment. His head bucked. "Exactly. Sergeant Mayfield, conduct Mr. Marshak to my office. Rest of you—Kime, Mossman, I'll expect you there also. Within five minutes."

Pivoting stiffly, Denton strode briskly toward headquarters followed closely by Francis Kime and Mossman.

"When you're ready, sir," Mayfield said gently at Marshak's elbow.

Silently Jeff complied, and with the noncom beside him, struck off in the wake of the others. Anger was a strong current within him; anger at Marcie Denton, at Mossman, but directed mostly at himself.

He should have known better, not taken any chances on jeopardizing his position. He'd recognized in Denton an officer overconscious of rank and jealous to the extreme of his prerogatives—just as he'd known Marcie Denton was trouble the moment he'd met her. He should have used care with the father, stayed clear of the daughter; he couldn't afford to get sidetracked; the mission was far too important.

Jeremiah Denton was hostile and defiant as it was; now, with this stupid, fancied wrong to Marcie prodding him, he'd use it as a means for exercising his authority, perhaps even do an about-face on his promise to provide the escort. It would all be straightened out, of course, when Marcie explained the incident—but it would be like Denton to drag the matter out for days just for spite. And delay was one thing Jeff couldn't—

"Right here, sir," Mayfield said unnecessarily, his words breaking through the irritation that gripped Marshak.

Jeff turned into the walk, mounted the steps and entered the building, still airless with its trapped heat. The noncom, following orders to the letter, escorted him to the door of the commandant's office, halted, saluted.

"The pris'ner, sir."

Denton, rigid, face flushed, stood behind his desk. Mossman and Kime were near the window. The major bobbed his head curtly.

"Tell the post surgeon I want to see him, Sergeant. On the double."

Mayfield saluted, wheeled, pulled up short. "He's coming now, sir."

Lockwood entered the room, glancing curiously at Marshak. Denton pinned him with his eyes.

"How is she?"

"All right," the surgeon said. "Hysterical. I gave her a sedative. She's resting."

"Was—has she been harmed?"

"Apparently not. Frightened, I'd say."

Denton sank into his chair. "Very well. Thank you, Major. That'll be all."

Lockwood turned, left the room, closing the door as he departed. Denton bridged his fingers, stared at Jeff coldly.

"My duty," he began slowly, "is to warn you anything you say here now can be used against you at the court-martial. You understand that, Captain?"

Marshak met the man's steady gaze. "What I don't understand is the need for a court-martial," he replied tersely.

Mossman muttered under his breath. Denton's jaw tightened. "You deny an attempt to assault my daughter?"

Marshak's jaw sagged. "Assault? What kind of poppycock is that?"

"You deny it?"

"Of course I deny it. Ask the lady—"

"I saw it!" Mossman broke in angrily. "Don't try worming out. I saw her go into the stables with you. Then she came out—running, hair down, straw all over her clothing. You telling me I didn't see that?"

Jeff shrugged. "You saw what you saw," he said, containing his temper, "but your conclusions are wrong."

"What other explanation is there?" Denton demanded in a tone that indicated there could not possibly be any.

"I suggest you allow your daughter to clear this up. She can, easily."

Denton smirked. "That would be your answer. You heard the surgeon say she was under sedation."

"When she wakens."

"In all likelihood she will be in no condition to talk about it for some time—and I doubt if it will alter matters any. I also saw what Mr. Mossman saw, at least most of it. And facts speak for themselves."

"It's possible to misconstrue facts, which is what you're doing here."

"Hardly. Besides, there is something else involved—your striking a junior officer."

"To that I admit. I had cause."

"Cause?"

"Oh, call it discourtesy," Marshak said impatiently.

"That's a tin reason, Captain. Just what was this so-called discourtesy?"

Mossman said: "Sir, I can answer that. I called him a bohunk, and stated in effect that it was not possible to make one into an officer and gentleman."

Jeremiah Denton considered that with closed eyes, and then lifted his gaze to Marshak. "That true? Your antecedents of foreign extraction?"

"Polish."

"And you object to being reminded of it?"

"Not to the fact that I'm Polish—which I'm not. I'm an American born in New York of Polish parents. It's the inference that there's some taint to it."

Denton drummed on his desk. "I wonder, mister," he said slowly. "I just wonder if it wasn't something else that caused you to strike Lieutenant Mossman. Could it be that when he confronted you after your misconduct toward my daughter you, in rage and frustration, struck him, knocked him down—"

"There's no—"

"And the term he applied to you had nothing to do with your actions at all?"

Marshak groaned. "More poppycock, Major—and you damn well know it!"

Denton's face flushed to deeper red. "Perhaps, Captain, but we'll see. We'll get to the truth at a court-martial. I'll have charges drawn, and when the Colonel returns—"

"Sir," Jeff cut in icily, "may I remind you that I'm under strict orders to continued my mission."

"Orders be damned!" Denton roared. "You're under my command here, and you're up against serious charges. If necessary, I'll have someone else continue this mission of yours."

"I suggest you first check with Washington before making that decision," Marshak said, fighting to remain calm.

"You suggest nothing, mister!" the post commander snapped, coming to his feet. "Consider yourself under arrest. Sergeant!"

The door opened instantly and Mayfield stepped into the room. "Yes, sir?"

"Mr. Marshak is confined to quarters," Denton said, then glancing to Mossman, amended, "No, place him in the guardhouse. I want no more trouble while he's awaiting court-martial."

"Yes, sir."

Denton swung his attention to Jeff. "Charges will be drawn up tonight. They'll be presented to you in the morning. Meanwhile—I'll take that pouch containing your orders."

Marshak stiffened. "They can be of no use to you. I think it best they remain in my possession."

"I'll have them, Captain," Denton said, deadly quiet. "Either hand the pouch over or I'll have it taken from you forcibly."

Jeff's shoulders went down in helpless resignation. "Very well, Major, but before this charade goes much further, I suggest you speak with your daughter."

7

Promptly at nine o'clock that next morning Francis Kime, accompanied by First Sergeant Mayfield, appeared at the guardhouse. Marshak, after a restless night during which the seriousness of his position grew more apparent to him, rose to meet the young officer. There was only one cell and he was alone.

"Well, Lieutenant?"

Kime, his features comically solemn, cleared his throat and unfolded a sheaf of papers while Mayfield stood at attention in the doorway.

"Captain, I have to read you this list of charges and specifications. The rule you know . . ."

"I know, and consider them read. What about the Major's daughter? She make a statement?"

Disconcerted, Kime swallowed hard. "But I have to read—"

"The hell with that, Lieutenant! I know what Denton's cooked up. What about his daughter?"

"Hasn't said anything yet."

Marshak swore. "Still under sedation?"

"Wouldn't know. Nobody's seen her."

"Well, I want to see her! Take that message back to the Major. Tell him I demand she face me—with him present."

"But I—"

"Don't give me any trouble, Kime!" Jeff snapped, thoroughly aroused. "I've taken all the pushing around I intend to. I'm not letting any little two-bit tin god of a—"

Marshak caught himself. No sense making it worse, even less in taking his ire out on Francis Kime. He leaned forward, wrapped his fingers around the bars of the cell.

"Just tell him what I said, Lieutenant—as a favor to me."

Kime nodded, started an uncertain salute, abandoned it, and spun about. Reaching the door he hesitated, looked back.

"If there's anything I can do, Captain—make you more comfortable—"

"Only thing that'll make me comfortable is to get out of here and be on my way."

The young officer bowed his head and with Mayfield in tow, returned to the street. Jeff heard the sergeant say something to the guard posted outside, and then all was quiet.

For a time Jeff remained leaning against the grill, eyes on the rough planks making up the closed door. He hadn't expected matters to go this far, had been certain Marcie Denton would have cleared him by that hour. Why was she holding back? Bitter and weary he turned, sank onto the cot placed against the rear wall.

He hadn't been too upset about Carey Mossman and any charges referring to him. Mossman, when all was said, was a soldier and could be made to see reason when the urgency was explained. And Jeremiah Denton; he could be brought around, too. He might bluster and rant, but he wouldn't risk Washington's wrath with so thin a charge as that of one officer striking another.

It was Marcie not speaking up, saying the few words necessary to clear him that was beyond understanding. Why? It was hardly conceivable she'd still be in a state of mind that would prevent her from giving an accounting. What the hell was it all about, anyway? What was there to the witless incident that would throw her into hysterics? Anger and embarrassment, yes—but hysterics? The whole damned mess was ridiculous.

Pride. That's what it was. Marcie couldn't face up to rejection, to admitting to herself or anyone else that an offer of her affection was anything but welcome. But surely she wouldn't carry it to the point where she'd permit a man to stand court-martial over it.

Or would she?

Marcie Denton was a spoiled brat; there was no other way of putting it. Pampered, humored, allowed to have her head, she could not countenance defeat in any shape or form. And with her father in command of the post, odds were good she'd make him sweat out a stretch in the guard-house to satisfy her ego, if nothing else.

His one chance, if Marcie persisted in her silence, was the post's colonel. That, too, was a slim hope, however. Lock-wood had said the date of the senior officer's return to Fort

Whiterock was indefinite. . . . A message to Fort Craig. That could be a solution.

Colonel Canby was post commander at Craig—and he outranked Denton. Explain the situation to him, and if it wasn't possible to get this asinine court-martial thing quashed, at least arrange to have it postponed until he could complete the mission to Washington. Canby was high enough in military circles to see the urgency and recognize the necessity. . . . But how could he get such word to Canby?

Lockwood, the surgeon. . . . He seemed an honest, fair-minded man and probably no particular admirer of Jeremiah Denton. Write a letter, persuade Lockwood to somehow get it delivered to Fort Craig. . . . Marshak came to his feet, brushing at the sweat on his forehead. That was it—and by God, he had to do something! Couldn't just squat there in that damned cell and wait. The War Chest must get to Washington—too much depended on it.

"Guard!" he shouted, moving to the grillwork again. "Guard!"

The door opened. A private, musket held at port, peered in.

"Get the post surgeon over here."

The sentry looked over his shoulder. "He's in the CO's office. . . . Something's going on."

Hope lifted within Jeff. Colonel Searcy had returned perhaps. "What do you mean by that?"

"Can't say for sure, sir. Courier rode in few minutes ago. From Fort Craig. Then the Major called in all the officers. Everybody's rushing all about, seem in a powerful hurry."

"The Colonel there, too?"

"No, sir. Ain't seen nothing of him."

Jeff sighed. Probably dispatches—news of the war. "All right. But watch for Major Lockwood. When he comes out, call him over."

The enlisted man rested his weapon butt down on the step. "Ain't so sure I'm allowed to—"

"You won't get into trouble. Just tell the surgeon I've got a bandage that needs looking at."

The sentry nodded, satisfied, and closed the door. Almost immediately Jeff heard him sing out.

"Major Lockwood, sir. . . . Pris'ner's asking to see you. Something about a bandage."

The surgeon appeared, swiping at the sweat on his weathered features. He said something to the guard and pushed the door back until it was opened wide, then squinted at Jeff.

"What's this about a bandage?"

"Forget it. Had to give the guard a reason. What I wanted is to talk. . . . I need a friend, Major."

Lockwood grunted, leaned against the bars. "What I figured," he said. "What's on your mind?"

"Getting out of here—quick. I'm on special assignment and need to reach Washington at the earliest possible date—and Washington's a hell of a long way from here. Happens I carry orders signed at the top directing all officers to assist me in every possible manner. Denton's seen fit to ignore—"

"Little matter of a court-martial pending. More or less supercedes any orders—"

"Doubt that in my case, and there's absolutely nothing to the charges, anyway. Oh, I knocked Mossman on his butt for calling me a bohunk, but the girl—hell, you examined her, you saw she was all right."

"She hadn't been manhandled, if that's what you mean, and I'll so testify. She was hysterical."

"Nothing happened to bring that on, and I figure she'll clear me once she comes to her senses. But I don't have the time to waste hanging around. Here's what I want to do—get word to Colonel Canby at Craig, ask him to intercede—"

Lockwood was shaking his head. "Forget it, Captain. Too late."

"Too late!" Jeff echoed. "Why?"

"Courier just arrived from Fort Craig. Brought the word—we're to abandon Whiterock. Same order has gone out to Fort Buchanan and Fort Breckenridge. Everything's being shifted to Craig."

Marshak, momentarily stunned, recovered. "Means the court-martial's off, then," he said, relieved. "I can be on my way."

"Wrong again. Denton turned the papers on the matter over to the courier, along with other documents he was directed to forward, sent them back to Fort Craig. You're to remain a prisoner, face the charges when we get there."

Speechless, Jeff stared at the officer. Finally a groan slipped through his lips. "God damn Denton—he's determined to nail me to the wall! He's made it a personal issue."

"If it was your daughter maybe you'd take it personal, too."

"There's nothing to it—do I have to keep telling you that?"

"No," Lockwood said quietly, "you don't. I'm just pointing out Denton's position. And you're right about him. He doesn't like you, feels you've got unwarranted authority and that rubs him wrong. What did you say to him that's burning him so much?"

"Nothing, except what was necessary to make the pursuit of my orders possible. Showed him a letter from Washington—after he forced the issue—directing officers like him to comply with my requests."

"That's what it is. I know Jeremiah Denton from way back. He wouldn't take kindly to a captaincy having authority over his majority."

Marshak swore again. "Was a fool to rile him—and I tried to avoid it, but there was no time to lose. And now this thing with his daughter. I suspect he knows damned well there's nothing to it, but it hands him just what he wants—the means to crucify me so he can show Washington they can't ride over him."

Lockwood nodded. "Agreed—off the record, of course. Wish there was something I could do."

Jeff stared at the floor. "When do we move out?"

"Tomorrow afternoon late. The Colonel's expected in the morning. You thought of appealing to him?"

"Thought of it first off, but there seemed to be no assurance he'd get here any time soon. Sure, I'll place a request with him the moment he arrives. Hell, I'm willing to stand trial and prove I'm innocent if your Miss Marcie Denton won't own up to the truth—but I want it postponed until after I've finished my job."

"Not my Miss Marcie Denton," Lockwood said, scowling. "I'd have paddled her little round behind and straightened her out a good many years ago, if she were!"

The surgeon fingered his collar, drew himself erect. "Got to start collecting my gear. Denton wants everybody ready by noon. . . . Don't suppose there's anything I can do for you—anything reasonable, I mean."

Marshak shook his head. He held no fears for the hidden cargo in the wagon, and there was the possibility Denton would have him drive the rig, under guard, of course.

"Only one thing," he said as the officer moved toward the doorway. "When the Colonel gets in, make him understand that it's important I talk to him."

"Without benefit of Major Denton's presence, I presume."

Jeff grinned. "You're a wise, old man, Doc—and I'm obliged to you."

Lockwood grunted, winked and stepped out into the driving sunlight.

8

The morning wore on, with the brutal heat keeping pace. Marshak could hear the rumble of activity in the fort, but with the door again closed, could see none of it. The small opening in the rear wall of his cell was high and looked out over the steaming flats of the desert; the front of the guardhouse was several feet forward of the bars, and its similar window was equally useless.

Several times he heard riders pound onto the parade and wondered on each occasion if it signified the arrival of the post's colonel returning to take command of the evacuation. But no visitors came; either the senior officer had not put in an appearance, or Lockwood had failed to make known the request. Jeff doubted very much that Searcy, appraised of the matter, would ignore it.

Midday. . . . The interior of the guardhouse was like a furnace. Sweat-soaked and clothing plastered to his body, Jeff persuaded the sentry to leave the door open when an orderly brought his noon meal. It helped somewhat, but the change was negligible as no breath of air stirred from the seared flats.

He could see a small portion of the compound now, but it gave him little satisfaction. The area visible was a line of squatting huts used by the married enlistees and their families. Wagons had been drawn up before them, and men and women alike were engaged in loading possessions.

He began to worry about his own rig and its cargo. If the fort was short of vehicles it would be like Denton to order its load discarded to make room for what he deemed more essential. The wagon bed was now filled with provisions and water, personal belongings of his and the men who had made up the escort, along with extra harness, repair parts for the wagon, and a supply of grain for the mules.

Beneath all that, shielded by a false floor, was the all-important cargo—the War Chest. In all likelihood it would go undiscovered even if the vehicle were unloaded, but he disliked taking the risk. Someone might notice the weighted appearance of the wagon when it was apparently empty, or consider the shallowness of what looked to be a deep bed.

Three o'clock. . . . Four. . . . There had been no letup in the steady activity or the murderous heat. Nor had there been any sign of the colonel. Marshak, growing more incensed with each dragging minute, remained fixed to the front of his cell, with eyes, smarting from the glare, fastened on the narrow strip of compound visible to him.

Twice he saw Mossman and Kime hurry by, each intent upon some errand. Now and then a loaded wagon rumbled past, apparently assembling with others somewhere near the stables. Another hour. . . . The smell of cook fires began to ride the charged air. A kitchen orderly came, a different one this time, bringing a plate heaped with beans, chunks of boiled meat, and a cup of strong coffee.

Marshak stood back while the food was slid to him through the oblong opening in the bars at floor level. It couldn't be that the orderly would have to unlock the cell and enter, he thought bitterly; he'd then have a chance to make a break for freedom. Everything worked wrong. As the soldier turned to go, Jeff stepped forward.

"Corporal, I want to see the post surgeon. Get word to him."

"Can't be done, Captain—sir," the man said, not halting. "Major's got everybody busier'n a one-armed man dipping sheep, loading up."

"He'll see me. If you can't go, tell the guard."

"Ain't none. They got him loading wagons, too."

In the next moment he was gone, his boot heels beating a hollow tattoo on the baked parade. Marshak cursed feelingly, helpless in the throes of frustration. He kicked the food aside, kept only the coffee, and sat down on the cot. He must do something—he just couldn't sit there—and wait.

No guard was at the door. He wondered when the man had been pulled off; probably at noon. He swore again, thinking of the possibility of lost opportunity. Rising hurriedly, he crossed to the grill-like door of the cell, examined the lock. If he could somehow get a pry to working, or release the tumblers, he could get into the clear. In the confusion he'd never be missed, and it was not long until dark.

The lock resisted his every effort, and judging from the large number of scratches in the metal, others before him had made their try. Sweating profusely, temper now a surging throb within him, he gave up and returned to the cot.

God damn Jeremiah Denton and his prissy, addle-headed daughter! God damn Mossman and Kime and—yes, even Lockwood who'd failed to get his message through to the post colonel! If any one of them realized how important it was that he reach Washington—but he couldn't tell them, make them understand. Not all of it, anyway. He'd been sworn to secrecy and he had to stand by his oath.

No one came to collect the supper dishes. He considered that absently while he remained on the cot, eyes fixed, unseeing, on the rock-hard ground outside the door. Shadows were beginning to form and that was some solace; at least the heat would diminish, and with luck, there'd be a breeze.

Maybe Lockwood would come—or possibly even Colonel Searcy, if he'd arrived. Or young Lieutenant Kime. There was even a chance Marcie would show up, contrite and ready to clear him of the charges. He stirred, amused by that thought; Marcie Denton would never come.

He watched the lamps across the way go on in sullen silence. No one was coming—he'd as well make up his mind to that. He'd sit right where he was until time for the wagons to pull out, and then he'd be on his way to Fort Craig—in chains. Jeremiah Denton was relenting not one notch. He should know—

A sudden crackle of gunshots, mingling with shrill yells and the hard, quick pound of running horses brought Marshak to his feet. He leaped to his feet, crowded up against the bars, striving for a broader view of the compound. A woman screamed and then a half a dozen riders, bent low, flashed by the doorway.

Apaches!

Realization came with sickening force. Whiterock was under attack. He gripped the bars of the cell door, shook them violently, yelling with all the power in his lungs in hopes of attracting someone nearby.

Outside a glare began to fill the night. . . . Fire. The Indians were burning the huts and tents, possibly the loaded wagons, too. . . . His wagon. . . . He rattled the door harder, renewed his shouting.

More gunshots filled the lurid haze and somewhere on the

compound a confused bugler was blowing reveille. Another group of Apaches thundered by, smoke and dust swirling around them. Abruptly a figure was framed in the doorway—a thin, bent shape in a bloody, torn uniform.

"Kime!" Jeff shouted. "Get me out of here!"

The lieutenant, saber in one hand, pistol in the other, staggered into the room. The broken shaft of an arrow protruded from his right breast and blood was flowing freely from a wound in his head. He stood for a moment staring vacantly at Marshak, then stumbled toward the grating.

"No key . . ." he mumbled thickly.

"Pistol—use your pistol!"

Kime brought the muzzle of the weapon up to the lock, held it close and pressed the trigger. The room rocked with the blast and smoke boiled up in a swirling cloud. Jeff lunged forward, grasped the bars and wrenched savagely. Bits of shattered metal clinked to the floor and the door swung open.

Leaping through, Marshak reached the exit to the street. He paused, glanced at Kime leaning weakly against the bars.

"Come on—I'll give you a hand!"

The young officer shook his head. "As soon—make my stand—here. Luck—Captain."

Jeff nodded. "Luck to you, soldier," he said and plunged into the open.

Smoke lay solidly across the parade in black, suffocating layers, thickened more by the dust stirred into life by running horses. Marshak paused, threw a glance toward the stables. The pall obscured that end of the compound but he could see flames rising from several vehicles drawn up in a line nearby. They would spread quickly.

Immediately he started for that point, checked himself. Unarmed, he'd never get there. Wheeling, he raced for BOQ, flung open the door. The building was deserted but on the bunk he had chosen he saw his gear. Crossing hurriedly, he brushed it aside and dug out his rifle and the sack of cartridges issued him. He saw his revolver, snatched it up too, jammed it into its holster. Spinning on a heel, he returned to the street.

His papers. . . . Denton had taken them. He came around again, started for headquarters building, stopped. The structure was a seething mass of flames. Two figures lay on the walk. One was Denton, a lance piercing him through, the other looked like Sergeant Mayfield. Cursing, Jeff cut around and legged it for the stables.

Two Apaches loomed up in the smoke and dust. Both

swerved toward him, one with leveled musket, the other with upraised club. Marshak dropped to one knee, blasted the brave with the rifle from his saddle with one shot. The second was almost upon him. Leaping aside, he grabbed the Apache by the leg, dragged him to the ground. Using the butt of the Henry, he crushed the man's skull.

He hurried on toward the stables. Fires were increasing, but most of the fighting seemed concentrated below headquarters building at the end of the compound. He reached the vehicles nearest the stables and pulled up short. A rush of fear shocked him; his wagon had caught fire. Flames from a small shed had touched off a mound of loose straw; in turn the tongue and right front wheel of his rig had acquired the blaze.

Jeff looked around desperately. A farm wagon, partially loaded, waited a few paces beyond. It was light but it rode on heavy wheels and undercarriage. Without hesitation he rushed to where it stood, leaped into the bed and began to throw out the few items it contained. A wagonsheet was stretched lengthwise along one side. He ripped it away. A coffin. . . . He paused as a thought came to him.

There was no delay in coming to decision—duty lay uppermost in Jeff Marshak's mind. Seizing an ax he pried off the lid. A body wrapped in a sheet. He was glad the corpse was covered—no waxen face would haunt him in the nights to come when, and if, he survived to remember that moment.

Tipping the elongated box, he rolled the body onto the wagonsheet, and then dropping to the ground, he hoisted it to his shoulder and carried to a place nearby where the flames could not reach it.

Trotting back to his own wagon he began to transfer those items he felt necessary—grain, food, blankets, the cask of water, spare harness and wagon parts and the box of extra shoes for the mules. Almost finished, the quick drum of hooves reached him and he ducked low, hiding behind the shallow sideboards of the vehicle. Three Apaches rushed by, their dark faces grotesque with paint streaks in the eerie glow. They failed to note him, rode on, pointing for the racket at the far end of the fort.

Hastily he resumed his chore, and then satisfied he had all that would be needed, dumped the rest overboard and began to pry up the false bottom of the wagon bed. Relief ran through him when he saw the flat metal boxes and the cloth-wrapped bars, arranged side by side, just as he had placed them weeks ago in San Francisco. He had felt certain they would be safe, but seeing them dispelled any and all doubts.

Moving fast, he began to shift the cargo to the coffin, taking first the metal boxes and then the bars of gold. Their War Chest, the Californians had named it. He wondered what they would think if they knew it was being transported in a coffin—that he had usurped the resting place of a dead man, or woman, to give their bounty a safe repository. Like everyone else involved, they'd be happy as long as it got safely to Washington, he guessed.

The last of the cargo transferred, he replaced the lid, nailed it tight with the ax and turned to the stable. Fortunately the structure, while filled with a thin film of smoke, was yet untouched by fire. The Apaches could have avoided it purposely, he realized as he hurried down the runway, figuring to return for the animals and drive them off for their own use.

He found the mules, pawing and moving about nervously, led them quickly into the open, halting abruptly as several dim figures began to materialize in the murk.

"Get in there and turn them animals loose!" a voice bawled through the night. "Lively now!"

Jeff shook the fear that had swept him, beckoned to the noncom leading the detail. "Sergeant—give me a hand over here!"

The burly, soot-blackened man, clothing smoking in several places, wheeled immediately and trotted to where Marshak was beginning to back the team into position.

"Harness—there—" Jeff yelled, pointing to the pile of leather near his own vehicle, now burning furiously.

The sergeant dragged the straps and collars in close. Together they calmed the team, placed the harness and linked up the wagon. It was done quickly and with no lost motion. The old noncom, pinching out a tiny flame licking at his sleeve, faced Jeff.

"Anything else, Cap'n?"

The quiet composure of the man was a steadying rock in a swirling maelstrom. Marshak raised his hand in quick salute, feeling a lump of pride in his throat.

"That'll be all, Sergeant, thank you. . . . Better get out of here, quick."

"Yes, sir, Cap'n," the man said and wheeled toward the stables where horses were streaming out in frightened confusion.

Jeff, having a difficult time restraining the mules, sprang

to the seat. He paused long enough to get his rifle across his feet where it could be quickly reached, and then cutting about sharp, headed into the hazy depths blanketing the parade. The road, as he remembered from the map, lay due east of the fort. If he drove straight across, keeping well away from the lower end of the compound where all the fighting was centered, he should be able to make it into the clear.

Abruptly two figures broke through the pall on his right. Startled, he hauled back on the reins. . . . Marcie Denton. With her was Mattie, the housekeeper. Apparently they were trying to reach some point of safety on the opposite side—only there was no safety there, none anywhere in Fort Whiterock, in fact.

He opened his mouth to yell. The sound froze on his cracked lips as an Apache bolted into view, bore down on the two women with an uplifted ax. Marcie saw him, screamed as Marshak snatched up his rifle. Before he could fire, the Indian struck, cleaving the older woman's head.

Jeff fired. Blood blossomed on the Apache's chest and he went rolling off his pony to bounce like a rag doll in the dust. Marcie, still screaming, spun, started back for the center of the compound. Another rider broke through the gloom. Marshak fired again and as the Apache fell, shouted at the mules, wheeled them toward the staggering girl.

Coming alongside he reached down, caught her by the arm. Marcie's screams rose higher and she began to fight him blindly. He hung on grimly, fearful she would slip from his grasp, fall under the wheel. Leaning far over, he heaved with all his strength, dragged her into the wagon.

She dropped full length beside the coffin, her cries still tearing into the night. Jeff, bracing himself, fought the mules until they had swung completely about, and then let them run. Once underway he looked back over his shoulder. They were off the compound, out of the fort. And there was no one following.

9

Marshak, giving the mules their head, allowed them to run the fear from their bodies and then, a mile later when they began to tire from the breakneck pace, pulled them gradually to a halt.

Again he turned his attention to their back trail. The moon was strong and the land lay clear and sharp—and still devoid of pursuers. Thanks to the dense smoke and dust they had escaped unnoticed.

Marcie Denton's quiet sobbing reached him. He stepped over the seat, knelt beside her. She wore the same skirt and lace-decorated white shirtwaist he had seen on her that previous evening, but it was now streaked with soot, torn and scorched in many places. She lay where she had fallen, next to the coffin, displaced by the jarring, mad flight from the fort and almost crosswise in the wagon bed.

Slipping an arm under her shoulders Jeff raised her to a sitting position. He had no kind thoughts for Marcie Denton, the memory of what she had caused him still fresh in his mind, but she was a woman and she'd been through hell.

"You're safe," he said gruffly.

Eyes glazed, she stared at him. "Safe. . . . Where?"

"Road to Fort Craig."

It all seemed to come back to her in a rush. She started, half rose, a wild look coming into her features.

"My father—he's—"

"Nothing we can do for him—or any of them."

The trembling of her body slowly faded. She studied Marshak quietly. Then: "How did I get here? I—I don't understand. . . ."

"Saw you crossing the parade. There was an Apache. Got to you in time."

She lowered her head. "Are they all dead?"

"Probably."

"A massacre—but you escaped."

There was a thread of accusation in her tone. He drew away, rested himself against the wagon's low sideboard.

"I'd have stayed if there'd been any use. There wasn't."

"You ran," she insisted dully, getting to her feet. Turning, she gazed at the pale glow to the west. "I'm going back."

"Don't be a fool!" he snapped. "Apaches'll be there till daylight. You'd be dead the moment you set foot on the compound."

"You won't have to take me. I can walk."

"Forget it. Climb up on the seat. Got to tie down this load."

Pivoting, he dropped to the ground. She did not stir and he saw she was staring at the coffin, apparently noticing it for the first time.

"No corpse in it," he said, and waited for her to get out of his way. When she continued to stand motionless he reached out, jerked at her skirt angrily. "Move!" he barked impatiently. "Want to be as far from here as possible by sunrise."

Reluctantly, she crawled onto the seat. When she was in the clear he tugged at the coffin until it was again in the center of the bed, and then rearranging the balance of the load, took a coil of rope, cut off two equal lengths and lashed all securely into place.

He spent another five minutes carefully checking the mules and their harness, and finding everything to his satisfaction, climbed onto the seat beside her.

"I insist you take me back," Marcie said.

Her tone was peremptory, reminded him vaguely of Jeremiah Denton. He shrugged, put the mules in motion.

"Like I said—forget it."

"I won't—and I refuse to go—"

He whirled to her, savage in his impatience. "Look, I don't like this any more than you do! But I'm stuck with you and I'm forced to look after you until I can get you off my back! Now—I'll hear no more about it."

She was silent for a full minute. "What do you intend to do?"

"Keep moving toward Fort Craig. Mesilla's out. When we get close I'll set you down some place where you can get a ride to the fort."

"You won't stop there?"

His features were taut. "Thanks to you, I can't. Those charges your father filed—remember?"

"He's dead," she said woodenly. "That's all over with now."

"Hardly. He sent the papers on with the courier. The whole thing's there waiting for me." He paused and the lines of his smoke-darkened face grew deeper. "Was a hell of a thing to do to a man."

Marcie Denton looked down, folded her hands in her lap. "I didn't mean for it to go so far. My father—"

"Your father," Marshak cut in, "grabbed onto the idea and made the most of it. He didn't like me and he had a big hate going for the higher-ups in Washington, the men he thinks put him out here to rust. Figured it was a good chance to get back at them."

"He was my father," Marcie said quietly. "And I won't speak ill of the dead."

"Doesn't bother me a damn. I don't enjoy being crucified to satisfy another man's gripe—or some silly woman's whim—especially when it interferes with a job I've got to do."

She gazed out over the silvered desert, ghostly with its gaunt cacti, shadowy hollows and scrubby brush clumps. She began to weep softly.

"This job," she said, haltingly, "I—I didn't mean to interfere. I'm sure my father didn't. . . . It was just that I—we didn't understand."

Her tears did not soften him. "He understood. He saw my orders, and the letter from Washington that I carried—took them, in fact. They're lost now, burned."

Just how he'd manage without his papers Jeff Marshak was uncertain, but he'd do it somehow. Fortunately the money he'd been issued was safe in the belt strapped around his waist.

"Will you be able to go on?"

He nodded, eyes straight ahead. "No choice."

"Is—is it so important to you?"

"To me and a lot of other people. I was assigned—trusted to get the job done. Intend to do it."

"My father said you had a letter from the Secretary of the Treasury, or someone like that."

"He tell you what it said?"

Marcie shook her head.

"It's what riled him most, I guess. Was countersigned by General Scott. Suppose me being just a captain and him a major rubbed him wrong."

"Think what you will, he was a good officer—and a fine man."

Marshak made no reply, having his own ideas on the matter. He scrubbed at his chin and jaws, beginning to itch from razor neglect. A beard would just have to grow. All his personal items were ashes now back in the charred rubble of Fort Whiterock.

The mules trotted tirelessly on through the cool night. Occasionally coyotes sounded their querulous challenge from distant knolls and more than once their passage frightened long-eared jackrabbits into frantic flight. Jeff remained silent, tried to recall his map again, remember if there were any settlements near Fort Craig where he could rid himself of Marcie Denton.

Socorro. . . . That was the name of a close-by town. He'd leave her there and she could catch one of the supply wagons making a daily trip. Too bad Mesilla was out; it was a lot closer.

He looked ahead. The land was breaking up, dropping off into steep-sided arroyos and low, dark-faced buttes backgrounded in the distance by round-top hills. The iron tires of the wagon wheels began to make a slicing sound as they cut into loose sand, and the mules slowed.

They were leaving the hard-baked soil of the desert, entering a ragged area that would make for slow travel. He shifted on the seat, wishing he had forethought to lay a folded blanket across the hard boards, and leaned the Henry rifle against his leg. Next time they stopped he'd remember. There was no rule that said a man had to be uncomfortable.

"If you want to go to Fort Craig," Marcie said, apparently still thinking about the trouble she'd caused, "I could talk to the commander there, explain the charges were a mistake, ask him to drop them."

"You know the Army better than that."

"But if I told him—"

"Still cause a delay. Once you set machinery like that in motion, all hell won't stop it until it's run a full course. And I can't afford to hang around, wait."

"You keep saying that—you can't wait! It's a fixation with you—like a madness! Why is there such a hurry? Why is haste so important?"

He was looking beyond the mules, eyes on the road now falling away into a narrow channel running between walls of rocky ledges.

"Less you know of it the better."

She motioned at the coffin. "That has something to do with it, doesn't it?"

"It's a part of it," he said grudgingly, "but only a part. When we get to Socorro you'll be on your own, forget all about everything."

"Except my father, and Whiterock—and all the others," she murmured.

"He died in the line of duty," Jeff said, mustering the best he could from his store of kind thoughts. "Expect that's the way he wanted it. . . . If you're asked how you managed to reach Socorro, tell them you caught a ride in with a rancher."

His words faded suddenly. Two faces—strangely familiar faces—rose from the rocks on either side of the road. Fear jolted him solidly as he snatched at the rifle against his knee.

He had it half raised with twin orange spots blazed before him in the night and a shocking wave of blackness overpowered him.

10

Sometime during the chill, early hours Jeff Marshak stirred. Pulling himself to his elbows, he tried to rise. A gush of pain sickened him and he fell back, drifted again into a netherworld of soft darkness.

It was light when consciousness returned once more. He lay motionless, face down on the sand, struggling to collect his loosely scattered senses. But thought and remembrance came slow and with effort. He had been driving the wagon. . . . Two faces appeared among the rocks—familiar faces. . . . He had reached for his rifle. . . . Then had come two quick gunshots. . . . Nothing more. . . .

The wagon. . . . He sat bolt upright, the full import of what its loss meant striking him a hammer blow. Nausea rolled through him at his thoughtless, sudden motion. He twisted about, sagged weakly and retched.

More cautious when it was over, he pulled himself to his feet, stood swaying. The rifle had been trapped beneath him when he fell, lay now partly buried in the loose sand. Slowly, carefully he knelt, picked it up, brushed at its mechanism with his fingers.

Those faces. . . . The blurred edges began to fade and

abruptly they became definite. Wade Krause and Ross Conroy—two of his escort. . . . But they were dead! A grimness settled over him. Dead—hell! They'd deserted when the Apaches struck, somehow gotten away—and then lain in ambush for him.

He glanced about. There was no sign of the wagon, of course. Krause and Conroy had taken it, hurried off into the night leaving him for dead. Evidently they had planned to hijack the War Chest from the start, had been waiting for an opportune moment. The Apaches had upset their plans—or possibly it had come as a lucky break for them.

Goddamn them both to hell! Marshak trembled with fury, took an uncertain step forward, eyes fixed on the deep grooves left in the sand by the wagon's wheels. They wouldn't be hard to follow—and follow them he would, straight to perdition if need be.

He staggered on, vaguely aware of the sun's first slanting rays spraying out in colored fingers across the pearly dome of the sky. They had a good start on him, and they'd move fast; but they'd never get away from him, damn them—never!

He halted, staring at the tracks curving now to the right with eyes that did not focus too well. "Mexico," he mumbled. "Bastards are headed for Mexico."

Reaching up, he rubbed at his head which seemed oddly detached from his body, flinched as pain stabbed him sharply. Exploring cautiously, he felt stiffness on the skin of his left cheek and down his neck, realized it was crusted blood. There was more on his shoulder and chest. He'd bled to beat hell. The bullet, slicing across his scalp just above the ear, had clipped a vein when it knocked him cold.

Lucky. . . . He'd probably dropped like a sledged steer when that slug had hit him and blood started pouring from the wound. Krause and Conroy had figured him for dead, a bullet in the brain, otherwise they would have made sure. Marshak bared his teeth in a mirthless grin. They were due for a jolt; he'd be coming back from the dead the same as they had.

He should have expected something like this, camp scuttlebutt being what it was; he should have known he couldn't keep the purpose of the mission a secret—there was no such thing as a secret in an Army base. He should have remembered that, and remembered, too, there were always the Wade Krauses around.

He was a bit surprised at Conroy. Ross had seemed a straight sort of soldier, not smart, not dumb, just the average enlistee serving out a hitch. Funny, he'd never noticed Conroy hanging around with Krause; usually it was Noah Rudd. Probably Rudd had been in on the scheme, too, only an Apache arrow or bullet had taken him out of the picture.

Maybe they were all in on it; Mills, Bucknell, Ambrose Kennerman—even Amos Miller, but that was hard to believe. The noncom never liked Krause, nor did any of the others except Rudd. Gold, however—a lot of gold—often made bedfellows of even confirmed enemies.

He was slumped against the low embankment of a dry watercourse. He lay there, wondering how it happened, and when. He couldn't recall falling, or halting, but he had. He glanced at the sun. It was well on its way and bearing down with a merciless intensity.

Muttering impatiently, Marshak got to his feet. He felt stronger and the pain in his head was not so severe, but now he was beginning to notice the heat and a need for water. He moved up and out of the arroyo, looked ahead, following the wagon tracks with his eyes as far as they could reach. Whatever had occurred, he'd managed somehow to stay on the right trail.

He brushed at the sweat misting his eyes, resumed the march. The deserters would stop at the first village once across the border; they'd think themselves safe, halt to celebrate with a few drinks and maybe have themselves a meal.

The girl!

God in heaven—he'd forgot about Marcie Denton! They'd have her, too, thanks to him. But she'd be dead right then if he hadn't snatched her up, got her away from the massacre at Fort Whiterock. That might be better than being in the hands of Wade Krause and Conroy—but he'd not worry about her. She'd be safe until they were across the border.

Doggedly he followed the neat, twin grooves in the sand that, like powerful magnets, drew him deeper into a blistered land of scourged waste. He noted little of it, simply pressed on through the fields of emaciated cholla and spherical snakeweed, the iron-hard muscle and bone of the man's superbly conditioned body matched equally by his inflexible determination.

Midday found him on a small mesa studded with knobs of black lava rock. A short time later when he reached a larger of the countless arroyos, he halted in the thin shade of a yellow-flowered palo verde tree to rest.

But the pitiless drive within Jeff Marshak would not let him tarry long. Within a quarter hour he was again on his way and soon was crossing a crusted alkali flat that stretched, glaring white, in all directions as far as he could see.

Eventually he came to its edge but the arduous miles and the brutal sun had taken their toll. His steps were less purposeful. His vision was blurring and he became aware of a pronounced weakness in his sweat-clothed body.

He found it necessary to rest more often as the heat of the furnace through which he was passing became more intense. But he kept stubbornly at it; walk, rest, walk again—he repeated the monotonous routine until he declined into a sort of hypnotic catalepsy.

Thirst had long since become unbearable and every ounce of his dehydrated being clamored for moisture. Several times he glanced toward the shadowy mountains far to his right, toward those even more distant on his left. He'd find water there—a cooling spring, a clear, running stream; but to turn aside would mean extra miles and cost hours. Upon each occasion, when temptation sought to alter his direction, he shook it off, clinging tenaciously to the purpose that drove him on.

He fell when he was crossing a narrow hogback. He went down hard on the flinty rocks, bringing blood from half a dozen cuts and scratches on his hands and arms. Ignoring them, he struggled to his feet, continued.

Marshak noticed the loss of his pistol a few moments later, returned to examine the ground where he had fallen. It was not there. Either he had lost it back on the road when the deserter's bullet had knocked him from the wagon, or at some point later when he was crossing the desert. It was possible, too, that either Krause or Conroy had taken it. He was not troubled; he still had his rifle.

At last the sun was dropping lower. In a few more hours it would fall behind the ragged horizon to the west and traveling would be easier. . . . If only he had water—just a mouthful to ease the fiery craving that tortured his throat. But there was no water anywhere in that seared garden of hell. His one hope was a rain shower, and the brassy sky gave no promise of that.

I can't go much farther.

The thought worked its way insidiously into his brain, began to gnaw at his consciousness until it was a banner waving frantically in his mind. He fought, continually refusing to accept what he knew was inevitable. The sun would go down. . . . It would be cooler. . . . Thirst would ease. . . .

He'd make it. . . . By God—he'd beat them all; Krause, Conroy, the sun, the heat—the desert. He'd beat them!

Stumbling, he fell. Releasing a deathlike grip on his rifle, he tried to rise again. His arms gave way. His red-rimmed eyes rolled to the back of his head and he went flat on the hot sand. His strength was gone.

The sun had disappeared when he again stirred. Rolling wearily to his back, grateful for the faint breeze slipping through the night, he stared at the star-bright sky. Alarm filled him and he staggered to his feet. He had to keep going. . . . The wagon—the cargo.

Moving unsteadily he lurched forward, eyes searching for the telltale tracks of the wagon's wide wheels. They still bore directly south. Relieved, he grunted, went on. His muscles had turned stiff on him during the respite and walking had become painful, but he ignored again the discomfort, stumbled on, gaze fixed on the rim of a gentle rise lifting before him.

Short of the crest he halted. He had thought traveling would be easier when the sun had gone, but realized now heat had not been his only enemy. A leaden weariness, spurred by thirst and a sullen hunger, had risen to torment him. He denied them all, soon resumed the tedious climb, making use of the rifle as a staff to assist his faltering steps.

Abruptly he halted. He was on the summit. Off in the distance, lights winked feebly in the half-dark. Marshak stared vacantly at the tiny, yellowish dots, and then comprehension swept through him.

A settlement!

He'd made it.

11

One lamp still burned in the village when he finally reached the outskirts. From the top of the rise it had appeared no great distance to the settlement, but the clear, starlit night had deceived him. It had required hours and an endless succession of miles, it seemed to him.

Exhausted, sagged against the crumbling ruins of an adobe wall, he focused his eyes on the silent collection of huts. Several trees near center, surrounding a circular formation of rocks, caught his attention. Water. . . . Croaking harshly, he half ran, half stumbled to the well.

He wasted no time lowering the wooden bucket hanging from a frayed rope. A horse trough, filled to the brim, offered instant relief. Dropping to his knees he plunged his head into its cooling depth, taking long, satisfying gulps while he dashed handfuls of water over his neck and torso.

He hung there for a full half hour while strength returned gradually to his body, and then finally drew himself upright. A dog began to bark somewhere to his left and he cursed at the ill luck of having aroused the animal. But after a few moments the racket ceased and he reckoned the dog had been disturbed by something other than his arrival.

Moving out from beneath the trees, Jeff walked unsteadily but quietly through the shadows cast by the huts. The solitary light he had noted appeared to be deeper in the village. He came upon it shortly, a squat, somewhat larger structure than the others. CANTINA, the sign over the door stated.

Anxiety began to tag his mind. The wagon was nowhere to be seen. Could he have made a mistake? Had Krause and Conroy avoided this village, chosen another? The wagon's tracks had led on—his thoughts came to a dead stop. He hadn't actually followed the sandy ruts after spotting the lights; he had rushed on, blindly assuming he would find the deserters in the settlement. For all he knew they could have swung off.

Cursing himself for such stupidity, he continued, approaching the saloon in muted, carefully placed steps. The dog had begun to bark again but he gave that no consideration. Reaching the corner of the building, he halted, threw his glance to the rear. Relief poured through him. The wagon was there, pulled in behind the structure.

In a dozen long strides he reached it, made a hurried inspection. The position of the coffin had been altered—an indication that it had been examined by the outlaws. Looking closer, he saw that the lid had been removed and replaced. Evidently Krause and his partner decided the long box was a good disguise and elected to make further use of it. Typically, they had not taken the trouble to lash it back into position.

Grim, tension now building within him, he cracked the Henry's action, made certain a cartridge was in the chamber, and retraced his steps to the front of the building. The door stood open. Keeping close to the wall, he worked his way to a point where he could look into its dim interior.

Krause and Conroy, Marcie Denton between them, sat at a table in a back corner. Food and a bottle of liquor was before them. Krause was speaking. His mouth was full and overflow was stringing from the corners of his lips, adhering to the beard stubble on his chin. Ross Conway ate steadily, merely nodding now and then. Marcie, rigid and seemingly paralyzed, looked straight ahead, her food untouched.

To their left the saloon's proprietor, head on folded arms, dozed at a crude bar. The only lamp in the place was in a wall bracket nearby. Marshak couldn't see the extreme front corner of the room, but he doubted if there would be any other patrons at that hour.

Cool, anger sharpening his faculties, Jeff studied the situation. The girl was in a bad position, trapped between the two men. He'd have to be careful; she could, in sudden fright, leap up, get in the line of fire. . . . He shrugged off the possibility, glanced over his shoulder. No one around. Lifting the rifle, he muffled the cocking of the hammer with a cupped hand, laid the barrel across his forearm and stepped into the room.

"Krause! Conroy!" His voice had the crackling quality of a mule-skinner's whip.

The pair came to their feet as one. The table tipped, crashed to the floor with a clatter of dishes as Marcie uttered a piercing scream. Conroy brought up his pistol in a quick, blurred motion. Marshak triggered the Henry, saw the deserter slam back against the girl and start to sink as he spun to fire at Krause ducking behind the bar.

"Qué pasa? Qué pasa?"

The Mexican saloonkeeper's shrill cry rose above the echoes rocking the smoke-filled quarters. Krause's head bobbed into view at the far end of the counter. Jeff snapped a bullet at the fleeting target, strode deeper into the room. He reached the corner where Marcie, hand pressed to her lips, eyes spread with terror, cowered against the wall.

"Come on!" he shouted. "No time to waste!"

Gunshots would bring onlookers—possibly even soldiers. The Mexican Government usually kept a contingent of *Rurales* bivouacked in settlements along the border, and he wanted no encounter with them.

Marcie remained frozen, unable to stir. Cursing impatiently, Marshak stepped nearer, savagely kicked aside the table and seized her by the arm. Yanking her forward, he wheeled, began to back toward the door.

Wade Krause appeared at the end of the bar, a pistol in each hand. Marshak thrust Marcie to the side, aimed hurriedly. The bullet splintered a shelf on the wall behind the outlaw, exploded a small cloud of dust. In that same instant Krause brought his weapons into use.

Jeff heard slugs rip into wood beyond him, lunged to the right for a better shot at Krause. He saw the man, prone, only head and shoulders visible. Pivoting fast he got off two rapid shots. Krause yelled, disappeared.

Marshak stepped back, reached for the girl's arm, and lunging by the stricken barkeeper, hurried into the open.

The village had come alive with lamps, and voices were shouting into the night. Several dogs had taken up the cry, and beyond the *cantina* Marshak could hear the hard pound of oncoming boots. Hanging tight to Marcie's hand, he crossed the front of the building, raced its length to where the wagon waited.

"Climb up—hurry!" he shouted, pushing her at the vehicle as he halted to free the mules.

The rope came loose at first tug. He spun, looped the trailing end in a harness ring, wheeled to leap aboard. Marcie Denton stood mute and motionless beside the front wheel.

"Goddamnit—move!" he yelled, and seizing her by the waist, threw her onto the seat.

He was beside her in the next instant, aware the rough treatment accorded her had aroused her somewhat, aware also of half a dozen men streaming around the corner of the saloon.

He cut the wagon in a sharp circle, reached for his rifle and pressed off a shot into the ground at the feet of the approaching men. They halted as dust spurted against them. More shouts went up. The mules, startled by the gunshot and yells, lunged into their harness. The wagon slewed half around, righted itself, sped on.

"Hold on!" Marshak warned the girl. "Got to make it to the border!"

He had no idea how far it was to the line. Less than a mile, he guessed, but he could take no chances; he'd leave plenty of margin—if they could reach it.

The rattling wagon, bouncing over the broken ground, skidding, sliding and perilously close to overturning several times, finally reached level surface. Jeff looked back. There was no pursuit—and there'd be none insofar as Krause and

Ross Conroy were concerned, he thought with deep satisfaction. . . . But there could be *Rurales.*

He shifted his eyes to Marcie. She sat in tense silence, one hand gripping the edge of the seat, feet braced against the dashboard. She was staring straight on and in the moonlight her features were pale and blurred.

The wagon dipped suddenly into an arroyo, slowed as loose sand caught at the wheels. They were below the plain and entering an area of broken hills and dry washes littered with rock and brush. Marshak breathed easier. Anyone following would have difficulty locating them in there; the rugged country, the darkness would combine to conceal their movements. Probably it didn't matter; he was certain they were well beyond the border.

12

Easing back to rest his tired muscles, Marshak studied Marcie. "You all right?"

She nodded woodenly, stiff and unyielding in her manner. "You killed them—both—shot them down."

He stared at her in astonishment, and then a furious impatience ripped through him. "What the hell should I have done—slapped them on the wrist?"

Marcie Denton continually confused him. At times she seemed sensible, capable, almost hard; on other occasions she struck him as soft, impractical and far out of her element in the raw frontier where he had met her.

"Had no choice," he said, his tone curt. "Otherwise it wouldn't have ended. They'd dog my trail all the way to Washington."

"Maybe not, when they realized—"

"You don't know their kind. Never give up—not them. Too much to gain."

He stirred angrily, disturbed that she would give the two deserters the slightest consideration. They had ambushed him, left him for dead; kidnapped her and made off with valuable property destined for important, vital use—and she felt sorry for them! What sort of woman was she?

"I know about your cargo—the mission."

Jeff was not surprised. He merely shrugged, held his eyes on the road twisting its way through the brush. They'd have to stop soon; the mules needed rest and a good feeding, as did he. Halt at first light, he decided, glancing to the eastern sky. They'd be a long way from the border by then.

"Gold, I heard them say. Two hundred thousand dollars worth, maybe more. They opened that coffin."

"They touch it?" he asked, suddenly tense.

"No, just sort of dug around, made sure it was there. They thought the coffin was a good way to hide it. Nobody would ever think to look in a coffin for gold."

The same idea, only with embellishments, had been rocking about in his mind. A couple—a man and his wife taking the body of someone—a relative, perhaps—to a settlement for burial. It made a pretty convincing story, and, as the outlaws had said, no one was likely to get suspicious and open a coffin. It would work fine except they were not dressed like a farmer or a rancher and his wife—and then there were those outsized U.S. brands on the mules.

"Your mission is to get that gold to Washington, to help with the war, isn't it?"

She was shivering, he noticed, and reached into the wagon bed for one of the blankets, laying it across her shoulders.

"That's it," he said, noncommitally.

She shook her head, expressing her doubt. "That's not all. Two hundred thousand dollars—not much where a war is concerned."

"It'll help."

"Possibly, but it doesn't make sense. All this trouble for so little—"

He swung his hard-cornered face to her. Crusts of blood still matted his beard in spots and his eyes were deep-set and glowing under their bony shelf.

"You've guessed it," he snapped. "Now, drop it!"

They had reached a small clearing, hemmed in on all sides by dense brush. He looked again to the sky fading to pearl-gray and drew the team to a halt. Marcie glanced at him questioningly but he turned away, dropped to the ground. The inbred courtesy of the man caused him to pivot, hold out his arms to assist her, but unmoving, she continued to stare off into the hills.

"Suit yourself," he murmured and stepping to the front of

the team, began to remove the bridles. He decided not to unhitch the mules from the wagon in the event a hurried departure became necessary.

Departure. . . . They'd been traveling more or less in a northeasterly direction, and he was remembering again the report that had been received at Whiterock. Confederate forces had moved up and occupied Mesilla and the area surrounding it. Undoubtedly the men of the South would fan out, extend that occupation westward. Chances for encountering such patrols were disturbingly good.

He fed and watered the team, using nosebags for the grain and the bucket provided for water, and noting absently that Marcie had finally climbed down from the seat and was standing at the side of the wagon. She was taking no interest in his activities, appeared to be waiting only for the moment when they would continue the journey. He smiled quietly. She'd not be happy when he told her of his plans for the future.

"Hungry?" he asked, making an effort at cheerfulness as he moved to the wagon and began pulling the provisions sack from the bed.

She moved her head slightly, drew the blanket more closely about her slender figure. "Cold more than anything."

"Have a fire in a few minutes," he said, and setting aside the sack, began to collect twigs and dry sticks. Jeff was careful in his selection—he wanted no smoke signal rising into the sky to attract passersby.

Once the flames were going he made coffee in a small lard bucket and warmed up several biscuits and some slices of dried beef.

"Not much of a meal," he said, still hopeful of breaking down the cool reserve with which she'd clothed herself. "Do better when we're out of this country."

Marcie accepted the cup of coffee he offered her solemnly, met his gaze. "When will that be?"

"Two, maybe three days."

She lowered her head, sipped at the steaming liquid. "We'll be near Fort Craig then."

"You won't be going there," he said bluntly, and awaited her reaction.

The full impact of his statement did not register for several moments. He thought she had not heard or possibly misunderstood, and then he saw her color pale as she placed the cup on the ground beside her.

"What does that mean?"

"Need your help, at least until I get to Rolla—a town in Missouri—where I can catch a train. You'll have to stay with me until then."

She leaned forward, eyes bright and snapping. "You expect me to do that?"

"Exactly. We'll get some clothes somewhere—pass as man and wife. We get stopped I'll say we're taking my brother to the next town, whatever it may be, for burial. Coffin will back up the story—"

"I refuse," she interrupted flatly, "and you can't force me to do it." Her voice rose. "You hear? I won't!"

Marcie's words were a defiant scream. He reached out, pushed her back. "You've got no choice," he said calmly.

"I can run—"

"To where? I aim to bypass all towns along the way. We'll never be near anything."

She began to weep. "I don't care—and I won't do it. . . . You have no right—"

"I've got every right!" he snarled, aroused. "If it hadn't been for you I'd not be in this fix. I could have followed my original plan, stopped at Craig and all the other camps along the way. . . . But you changed that for me—changed it so I'll have to avoid them."

"I—I offered to straighten that out—swear it was a mistake."

"You got that idea too late to do me any good. I'd be all summer getting myself in the clear—and I can't let that happen. I've got to get that cargo to Washington."

"I don't believe that, either. Two hundred thousand dollars isn't a drop where the Government is concerned."

He considered her through half-closed eyes. Perhaps if she knew the truth, not just part of it, she'd understand and be more cooperative. . . . And like it or not, she was a part of the mission now, anyway.

"Two hundred thousand—that's not even a quarter of what I'm delivering."

Marcie frowned. "But those men, they said—"

"They were going on rumors. All they knew was there was gold. Quite a lot of it."

"How much is there?"

"Over a million dollars."

Marcie Denton gasped. "But how can—"

"Not all gold, of course. Biggest part of it is in diamonds and rubies—emeralds—a lot of jewelry. All came from the people of San Francisco. They called it their War Chest and donated it to the Government.

"Biggest problem was getting it to Washington. No stage-coaches running, and they wouldn't be safe with the Rebels on the loose—not to mention Indians and outlaws. Boat would take too long, and that wouldn't really be safe either. So somebody came up with the idea of shipping it back by special courier, using a wagon. I volunteered for the job of getting it through. I figure to do it—no matter what it takes."

"Just you alone—and a million dollars."

"Wasn't that way at the start. I had seven men, all good, I thought. To anybody we looked like another Army supply detail headed east. You know what happened after we got in New Mexico.

"And I won't be alone now. You'll be with me, making out like you're my wife on a sad journey. It'll get us through to Rolla without any trouble."

"If I refuse—"

"You won't," Marshak said, features going cold. "Make up your mind to that. You're part of the job now."

She tossed her head. "You just think you can force me. . . . You can't watch me every minute of the day and night. I'll get my chance."

"To run? Where'll you go? We'll never be near a settlement, and we'll be crossing Apache and Reb country—at least until we're beyond Fort Craig. Then it'll be something else."

"I'm not afraid."

He grunted in disgust. "You should be. I sure as hell am."

"I'll manage. You'll have to stop for supplies. Maybe the wagon will break down. You won't have much luck keeping me prisoner—I promise you that."

He shrugged, gave up trying to make her see reason. "Have it your way," he said, rising, "but you'll be with me when we get to Rolla."

She was determined to have the last word. "I think not," she said coolly and turned away.

He collected the few utensils they had used, restored them to their box in the wagon and then kicked sand over the dying embers of the fire. He had hoped she would understand, work with him willingly on the task he had sworn to complete. It had been a waste of words.

But it changed nothing. Willing or not she would be with him; she had become a part of the whole, a factor in the mission—in reality, the answer as to how he could cross the next thousand miles or so in comparative safety.

Perhaps she would change as time passed. He looked forward with no relish to a continual battle with her in the weeks to come. I can hope, he thought, as he began to ready the mules.

The next thing necessary was to obtain suitable clothing and thus complete their disguise. He could blot the brands on the mules to some extent with mud. It might even be a good idea to swap them off, not take the risk of having them recognized. But finding someone willing to trade for Army property could be difficult—and there was a danger of arousing suspicion.

Finished with the harnessing, he moved to the wagon. Remembering an earlier thought he took another blanket, folded it into a cushion and spread it across the seat. Then, climbing aboard, he looked down at Marcie, stubborn and perverse, standing at the edge of the clearing.

"Pulling out," he said. "You can ride or you can walk. Makes no difference to me."

She flung him a flashing, angry glance and wheeling, mounted to the seat and sat down beside him.

"My time will come!" she said in a brittle, furious voice. "Wait and see!"

He shrugged, slapped the rumps of the mules with the lines. It would be a hell road all the way to Rolla, he could see that.

13

Taking bearings from the point on the horizon where the sun was beginning to show, Jeff Marshak headed the team due north. It would have been so much easier and shorter to continue east, angling across Texas, through the Indian Territory, and into Missouri, but that was out of the question.

The Confederacy ruled Texas and he lacked sufficient faith in the ruse he planned, and in his own good luck, to chance it. True, with no credentials now in his possession, he also stood to lose the cargo to Union soldiers somewhere along the route, but this would be a loss not so grievous. At least the California War Chest would fall into friendly hands and could, if all went right, eventually reach its intended destination. But it could involve months of delay and there was, of course, always the possibility of dishonesty somewhere along the line.

He couldn't let it end that way. He must complete the mission himself, for only that way could he be satisfied the job was done. A direct, single-minded man dedicated to a purpose once undertaken, he was finding it difficult to understand Marcie Denton's attitude; but he felt no compunction in forcing her to his will. He took no enjoyment from it, to be sure, but the emergency called for extreme measures and his insistence, therefore, was entirely reasonable.

Anyway—why was she so opposed to it? She was alone now, with nowhere to go, and she was Army with a knowledge of military problems and needs. It seemed to Jeff she should have been more than willing to assist in getting the War Chest to Washington, critically in need of gold to back the Government's issue of paper money.

The cost of war preparations had hit the country hard. Eighty million dollars, or near that, someone had told him, was the size of the Government's debt. And with a greater buildup in the military, it would increase. Gold was needed, and needed quickly. Without substantial reserves bankruptcy was inevitable.

The million the Californians had raised wasn't much—one eightieth of the debt when you got right down to cold figures, but it was a start; and it was believed that the example set by California would encourage other states as well as foreign sources to pitch in, throw their support to the Union.

But it had to be done quickly. It was dangerous to let the matter drag, allow any hint of financial weakness become apparent. Thus Marshak's orders had been specific in their reference to urgency, placing that second only to the need for completing the mission at all.

He lifted his eyes. A thin smoke plume twisting lazily into the heavens had appeared beyond a roll of hills in the distance. He thought back, tried to recall the map he had carried, and lost in the fire at Whiterock. He could remember no settlement in that particular area. Of course, he could be wrong; he was considerably south of where he had intended to be.

He glanced at Marcie, a quiet, graven image at his side. She had not noticed the dark stain against the sky. He said nothing of it.

Two hours later, with the sun well on its way and already making itself felt, they topped a rise and looked down not upon a settlement but upon a lone house squatting in a rectangle of undernourished land. It was a forlorn outpost, the bleached gray-green of it relieved only by a single tree flourishing in the overflow of a water well.

"Homesteader," Marshak murmured, pulling in the mules.

Marcie made no reply but he could sense the lift of hope within her.

"You're fresh out of luck," he said dryly, and pointed to a cloud of dust trailing a buckboard a mile to the east. "They've gone visiting—or maybe to town for supplies."

The girl's shoulders drooped and she bit at her lips. "It's Sunday. . . . To church, likely."

"No matter, makes it easy," Jeff said, putting the team into motion.

She looked at him. The hard angle of his jaw with its faintly red stubble of beard lent him a sort of prophetlike appearance.

"Why?"

"Clothes. Got to get rid of this uniform. And you need something more sensible than that outfit you're wearing—the kind of dress a farmer's wife would have on."

"This will do," she replied coolly.

He dropped the subject, concentrated on guiding the mules down the steep slope and into the yard where he drew them to a halt at the watering pond. Taking up his rifle, he faced her.

"What's it to be? I can tie you to the seat—"

Instantly she whirled, eyes blazing. "You'd do that, wouldn't you? Nothing means anything to you except getting through with that—that treasure!"

"You're right, nothing else counts. Thought you knew that by now. If it's necessary to lash you down every time we stop, like I've done that coffin, I'll do it."

She lowered her head. "I'll wait."

He nodded, swung from the seat and strode toward the house. He had little fear of her making an escape; the yard was a dead end and by the time she got the team turned around he could be there to stop her.

He reached the thinly boarded shack. That no one would be inside the structure he was certain, but he took a moment to knock. There was no answer to his summons. He tried the door. It opened with a dry squeal, and tossing a last glance at Marcie sitting in prim outrage on the wagon seat, he entered.

The folly of homesteading in an arid, sterile land was instantly apparent. The house contained only the barest necessities and Jeff felt a pang of guilt at being compelled to do what must be done.

Making his way through the small rooms and their makeshift furniture, he located a closet, began to rummage about in the few items hanging within. He found a hat, a worn pair of cotton pants and a fairly decent shirt. All looked a bit small but under the circumstances he could not be choosy.

For Marcie he selected a very plain calico dress of the type housewives wore while going about their daily chores. A ragged-brim straw hat looked to be a good prospect in protecting her from the sun, but a moment later he discarded it for a deep sunbonnet. The straw was more for working in the field; the bonnet would be better for travel.

Satisfied, he returned to the kitchen. On a shelf opposite the cast-iron stove were several jars of dried fruits and preserved meat. Taking down a few of each, he searched about for a container, eventually came upon an empty flour sack and made use of it.

Reaching then into his pocket he took two gold coins—far more than enough to pay for what he had taken—and dropped them on the table. With that he retraced his steps to the wagon.

Marcie sat as he had left her, rigid, lips compressed, eyes on the faraway hills. He added the food to the store in the wagon bed, tossed the dress and bonnet he had obtained for her onto the seat.

"I'm going over in the brush and change," he said. "While I'm gone—put those on."

He did not wait to hear her reply, simply moved behind a hillock of sand-buried greasewood. The pants were tight and the shirt bound his shoulders, promising to split at the seams at the first exerting effort he made, but they would do. The broad-brimmed hat fit fairly well.

Scuffing out a shallow pit with his toe, he buried the uniform, covered the scar with leaves and dry branches, and doubled back to the wagon.

Marcie Denton hadn't moved.

Anger went through him in a flaring gust. Striding up, he reached for her arm, dragged her roughly from the seat. Snatching the dress, he threw it at her.

"Put it on!"

Her temper matched his. "I won't—never!"

His arm shot out. Strong fingers fastened upon the shoulder of her shirtwaist. With a downward sweep he ripped it from her body.

Marcie screamed, fell back, covering her breasts with folded arms. "You—"

He took a long step toward her, hand reaching for the skirt she wore.

"Put it on!" he raged, "or by God, I'll strip and dress you myself!"

Eyes wide with fear, she tried to turn. He caught her arm, checked her. Abruptly Marcie wilted.

"All right," she said brokenly.

He picked up the dress where she had dropped it, thrust it into her arms, and spun to the wagon. Seething, he lifted the water cask, carried it to the well and filled it to capacity with cold, fresh water. Replacing it in the wagon bed, he stalked back to the overflow pond, scooped up a double handful of mud and spent another ten minutes covering the burned-in letters on the mules. When he had finished, Marcie was on the seat waiting. She wore the dress, the sunbonnet was in her lap.

He settled beside her. Still in the throes of anger, he pointed at the bonnet. "Use it. Sun's hot."

She gave no indication of complying, or that she had even heard. Temper, unreasoning and violent, again claimed him. He snatched up the bonnet, clapped it on her head.

"Wear it! I've got no time to bother with a sick woman. Keep it on while the sun's out."

Simmering, the knuckles of his hands showing white as they gripped the reins, he cut the mules about and headed the rig north.

A time later, movement to their right brought him to attention. Frowning, he studied the boil of dust intently. It could be the homesteader returning, or other travelers. If so, there'd be no problem.

But as they drew nearer he saw it to be several riders on horseback, half a dozen at least. They were moving due west at a leisurely pace and as Marshak watched they veered, approached on a direct course. The hair on the back of his neck began to prickle; the men wore the gray uniform of the Confederacy.

Tense, he reached down, placed the Henry rifle on the

floorboards of the wagon, covered it with a blanket. It would not be seen, yet remained quickly available.

"Reb cavalry," he said, glancing at Marcie. "I'll do the talking."

She gave him no answer but a tautness came into her features, and there was a change in the depth of her eyes; fear or triumph—he could not be sure.

"No tricks," he warned quietly. "You're the daughter of a Union officer. They'd be as happy to take you prisoner as they would me."

14

The patrol fanned out, advanced in a line. Strung across the road, they halted, effectively blocking any passage.

Marshak gauged them with a critical eye. Texas cavalry. . . . Young, green. . . . Uniforms clean, unworn. . . . A bearded first sergeant looked to be the only member with duty years behind him. The officer in command was undoubtedly a brand-new second-john, fresh from the Point. Like many other graduates, when the split came, he'd swung his allegiance to the southern confederation.

"Halt!" the lieutenant called unnecessarily.

Jeff, already in the process of bringing the team to a standstill, watched the troopers drift in to shape a circle around the wagon. The officer rode in closer. He was even younger than he had first appeared.

"What's wrong, Lieutenant?"

The officer touched the brim of his plumed hat, nodded politely to Marcie, and in a rich, southern drawl noticeable for its lack of r's, said, "Morning, sir and ma'am. Lieutenant Gerald Chambers, at your service."

Jeff nodded. "Something I can do for you?"

"Just a routine patrol. Been Apaches reported in the neighborhood. Might I ask who you are?"

"Not an Apache for sure," Marshak replied.

One of the troopers snickered. Chambers flushed slightly

and the old sergeant growled an order for silence in the ranks.

"Can see that," the lieutenant said. "Your name, if you don't mind."

From the tail of his eye Jeff was watching the noncom. He was kneeing his mount toward the mules, examining them critically.

"Castleman. . . . Jim Castleman. . . . My wife, Marcie."

"Right pleased to meet you folks," Chambers said, again touching the brim of his headgear. "You all live hereabouts?"

Marshak, unobserved, continued to watch the elderly sergeant while apprehension began to build within him. He might be fooling the second-john; he wasn't so sure of the noncom.

"Back over the ridge a piece," he said, jerking his thumb indefinitely toward the southwest.

Chambers nodded, rubbed at the beard striving for recognition on his chin. "Indians bothering you any?"

"Seen a few. No trouble."

"Good. Good. You and other folks around here won't have to worry about them much longer."

"That so?"

"Fact. Colonel Baylor plans to proceed with the wishes of you all, make a new territory of this part of New Mexico. Capital will be Mesilla." He paused, smiled broadly. "Ought to make everybody happy."

Marshak grinned. The Confederate leader was smart. That portion of the Territory, far removed from the seat of government in Santa Fe, had been trying for a year or more to break away and stand on its own. By acceding to their wishes Baylor would line the area up solidly behind the Confederacy. He became aware of Chamber's intent stare.

"I trust you're one of those in sympathy with the move?"

"Certainly," Jeff said hurriedly. "Everybody around here is. Might as well not be a part of New Mexico far as Santa Fe's concerned. Doubt if they know we exist."

He was only repeating something he'd read in a California newspaper—an account of a so-called convention held in Tucson months previous when the first clamor for separation was being voiced.

"Glad to hear that, Mr. Castleman. We're already moving forces into this part of the country. Soon have the Apache in hand."

The sergeant had evidently come to some decision on the mules. He now was circling the wagon at close range.

"Mind telling me where you're going?" Chambers question cut into Marshak's concern.

"Steins," Jeff replied, hesitating only briefly. Half turning, he pointed to the coffin. "Brother. Aim to bury him with the rest of the family."

The officer clucked softly in sympathy. "A sad duty. My condolences." He paused, said, "You refer, of course, to Stein's Pass."

"Some call it that," Marshak said, brushing quickly over what evidently was an error on his part. "Can't get used to calling it that myself."

"Your people have a ranch up there? Not much else around—no town as I recall."

It had simply been a remembered name on the map. Jeff had assumed it was a settlement. He nodded, smiled, hoped he was covering the slip.

"A ranch, yes. Folks are there." Matters were beginning to get out of hand. Best he break it off as quickly as possible. He glanced at Marcie, patted her arm comfortingly.

"If that's all, Lieutenant, we'll be moving on. Long drive ahead and my wife isn't feeling well."

Chambers pulled back hastily as if he had committed an unpardonable breach of etiquette. "Of course, sir! You're free to go—and my apologies to your lady for the delay. But we've got a war on, you know. Folks around here don't seem to realize that."

"All pretty far away. How is it going?"

"First-rate! We've just won a major victory at Manassas. Got the northerners on the run. It's expected our boys will shortly occupy the capital."

Shock ran through Jeff Marshak. A Confederate victory. It was hard to believe—and he wouldn't believe it, not without further proof. He lifted the reins.

"That's fine, Lieutenant," he said. "Now, expect we'd best be on our way."

"Mr. Chambers, sir." The old sergeant's voice was dry, raspy. "Mind asking the gentleman where he got them Yankee mules?"

Jeff felt Marcie stir against him in the tense hush that followed. Chambers, frowning darkly, cut about and moved in to where he could have a better look. Twisting about on his saddle, he faced Marshak.

"That's a U.S. Army brand on those animals, Mr. Castleman. Been smeared over with mud. You care to explain?"

Jeff grinned, made an offhand wave. "There a law says a

man can't grab onto a couple of Yankee mules if they're handy?"

Chambers clung to his stern expression. "You mean you stole them?"

Marshak shifted, spat. "Prefer to say I borrowed them, Lieutenant. Around here it's not considered stealing when it comes from the Yankees."

Several of the cavalrymen laughed. Chambers looked away, remained silent. The noncom drew up alongside the wagon, his sly old eyes narrowed and filled with suspicion.

"Reckon you won't mind none if I just look the rest of your things over."

Marshak tensed, forced a careless smile. "Help yourself."

"Never mind, Sergeant," Chambers cut in. "We've held these folks up long enough." Backing away, he touched the edge of his hat once more. "Good day to you, sir—ma'am."

Jeff, the tautness in his tall frame easing, slapped the mules smartly with the reins. "Same to you, Lieutenant."

The team broke into a brisk trot and began to pull away rapidly. "Don't look around," Marshak cautioned.

Marcie's voice was tight. "Don't you think they believed you?"

"Not sure. The lieutenant maybe, but that old top-sarge—I think he had a hunch things weren't right. Just couldn't put his finger on it."

"Will they follow?"

"Wouldn't surprise me, if he can convince Chambers. Got to try and throw them off."

Marcie Denton stared at the road running without deviation across a broad flat. "How can we lose them out here? They can see us for miles."

Jeff ducked his head toward a mass of blue-shaded mountains to the east. "Ought to start bearing for those hills pretty soon—if my map was right. Once we get there, we'll have a chance. Look now, see what they're doing."

Marcie turned her head slightly. "They've not moved."

Jeff swore softly. "Means that blasted noncom's trying to make Chambers see it his way. He wants to search the wagon."

"What could he find? They won't open that coffin."

"Couple of things that would be hard to explain. Military equipment—and my rifle. The Henry repeater would be a dead giveaway. Only a few of them issued, and all to the Union Army."

He raised himself slightly, tried to see the land beyond the bobbing ears of the mules. "Road bends toward the mountains a half mile or so. They still there?"

"Still there."

"Good. All we need is a little luck—and some typical second-lieutenant bull-headedness."

Marcie did not understand. "Bull-headedness?"

"Chambers is young, got himself a bright and shiny new commission. Go against the grain to take advice from a subordinate, no matter how much sense it makes."

They gained the curve in the road, shortly were entering rougher country where narrow, brush-choked arroyos angled off to either side. The trail itself, showing signs of considerable traffic, continued on, now slicing back and forth as it wound through steadily increasing buttes and masses of rock on its way to a breathtaking form in the crest of the mountain.

"Couldn't we pull off here, hide in one of these gullies?"

He shook his head at her suggestion. "That'd prove to Chambers we're covering up something."

Twisting, he then had his look. The lieutenant and his men were no longer in view, hidden by intervening obstructions. Immediately Jeff yanked the whip from its socket, began to lay it on the mules, sending them plunging ahead at increased speed.

"Once we make those rocks," he said, pointing with the leather-covered stock, "they can come. I can take care of them from there."

"Fight them—that what you mean?"

"Just what I mean. Place will be like a fort—and with a repeating rifle—"

The wagon began to sway. Marcie jammed her feet against the floorboards, braced herself with her arms.

"Maybe there's no need," she cried above the rattling of the vehicle.

Jeff didn't take his attention from the madly galloping mules. "Why?"

"What that lieutenant said—the South had won a big battle. Maybe they've already taken Washington."

"Doubt it. No reason to believe it's true. Can't see the Union Army folding that fast and easy. Anyway, takes more than one skirmish to win a war. Any sign of them?"

"No."

Marshak grinned. "Lieutenant Chambers is proud, no denying that."

The rock slides were just ahead. They gained the first

outcrop, wheeled by a bulging shoulder, rolled on through a steep-walled gash. The team was blowing hard and on the near-level ground Jeff pulled them down to a fast walk. The need for haste was over now; from that vantage point he could hold off double the number of men in Chambers's patrol.

"I see them," Marcie announced suddenly.

Marshak half rose, followed her leveled arm. Far to the west seven riders were moving slowly across the flat. He settled back satisfied. The officer was leading his men in an opposite direction in search of Apaches. Brushing the sweat from his face he turned, found Marcie regarding him closely.

"What's the matter?"

"Would you really have fought those men—those soldiers, if they'd come up the hill after us?"

"You're Army, you know the answer to that," he said laconically. "Like Chambers mentioned—there's a war on."

"But maybe it's over with. It could be, if the Confederates have captured Washington."

"It's not, far as I'm concerned. I'll keep on doing my job until I get proper orders to the contrary."

"But what if it is?" she persisted. "Then you'd be doing all this, making a long journey—killing several men perhaps, all for nothing!"

"Maybe's a word that doesn't count for much," Marshak said, "and I don't see things the way you do." He paused, gazed on the lifting, rock-ledged slopes rising before them. "We'll find a place up there to camp. Mules have about had it."

"So have I," Marcie said wearily.

15

It was near sundown, however, before the urgency within Jeff Marshak permitted him to cut off the road and seek camp in a grassy meadow a short distance below the crest of the mountain. There, sheltered by buttes and thick brush, he brought the team to a halt.

Marcie was near exhaustion. The long day, the previous night during which she had little sleep, and the terrible hours at Fort Whiterock, had taken the best from her. She was dozing when he stopped and he left her undisturbed on the seat.

He looked first to the comfort of the mules, never forgetting their importance and his absolute dependence upon them. There was ample forage where they had halted, more than enough to satisfy the animals, but if they were to withstand the long, grueling trip that lay ahead, they would need grain regularly. Thus, after watering them sparingly, he then attached their nosebags, generously filled. More water would come later.

When the mules were free of harness, picketed and munching contentedly, Jeff returned to the wagon. Quietly obtaining the necessary items for preparing a meal, he set himself to that task. He was chunking beef and potatoes into a spider for a quick stew when he heard Marcie behind him.

He glanced up. She appeared wan, had salvaged little rest from her nap. Pity stirred him.

"Supper'll be ready in a few minutes. After it's over you can get a good night's sleep."

She crossed to a flat rock on the opposite side of the fire, sat down, doing it woodenly, uncaringly. He put water to boil for coffee, and as a final treat, opened a jar of dried peaches—one he had procured earlier that day at the remote homestead.

The sun was gone before the food was ready, and the chill of higher places began to make itself felt. Marcie moved nearer, shivering visibly. Jeff added another handful of sticks to the flames, rose and obtained a blanket.

Draping it around her, he said, "Can't build up much of a fire. Rebs aren't the only ones we've got to watch out for."

She remained glum and silent, watched as he portioned out an amount of the savory stew onto a tin plate and handed it to her. Taking up a spoon she began to eat hurriedly, pausing only occasionally to sip at the strong coffee he had brewed.

When the meal was over, her spirits had risen somewhat, and although she said little, she did find it within herself to assist him in clearing the dishes and returning the supplies to the wagon where they would be safe from the small, nocturnal animals certain to visit the camp later.

Jeff watered the mules again, saw to their picket ropes and

retired finally to the fire. Digging a battered pipe from his pocket, he tamped it full with tobacco shreds, and stretched out.

Marcie Denton was there ahead of him, slender body hunched forward, eyes lost in the darting flames of the small fire. She had left the ridiculous bonnet in the wagon, and with the blanket drawn over her head, pinched in below her chin, she had the look of a lovely, golden-skinned madonna.

"You make a fetching picture," he said, puffing lazily at the blackened briar.

Her eyes touched him with a quick, concerned glance, returned to the fire. Jeff sobered as realization came to him. She was frightened—not so much of her surroundings and the possibility of marauders—but of him! He laughed, his tone carrying an ironic note.

"If it's your virginity you're worried about, forget it. I'm not interested in you except as a passport to Rolla."

The remark brought quick color to her cheeks, but when she looked at him he noticed the uncertainty had faded.

"Take my word," he added, still grinning, "the word of an officer and a gentleman."

He smiled then, recognizing the subtle meaning behind his statement. Picking up her cup, she pointed to the lard tin. "Is there coffee left?"

Marshak nodded. Folding his handkerchief into a pad, he filled her cup and poured a measure for himself. That done he grunted contentedly, resumed his sprawled, stretched-out posture.

"Can't remember when coffee tasted so good," Marcie murmured, looking off across the hills. "Do you suppose that young lieutenant and his men are out there somewhere?"

He pulled himself to one elbow, took a swallow from his cup. "Not likely. Be in camp by now. They weren't provisioned for overnight patrol."

Marcie was again gazing into the fire. She was thinking of Whiterock, he knew, perhaps reliving those last frantic, terror-filled minutes. It would do her good to get it out in the open, speak of it.

"You and Carey Mossman—were you engaged to marry?"

At once she was on the defensive. "Why?"

"No particular reason. Just conversation."

"I'm sorry," she said, lowering her head. "I guess you could say we were—not formally, just sort of an understanding." She hesitated. "Do you think any of them escaped?"

"Maybe. Have my doubts. Hell of a place to fight. Whoever called that a fort was—"

"I don't know how that got started. It was really only a camp on a temporary basis. When the Indians started making trouble Colonel Searcy asked for permission to move to Fort Buchanan. He knew Whiterock couldn't be defended if the Apaches decided to attack."

"Major Lockwood told me part of it. Searcy never got his approval?"

"That's where he was when you came—at Fort Craig. He'd gone to talk with Colonel Canby about it."

Marshak studied the smoke trickling upward from his lips. "Either he never got back or the decision to abandon Buchanan and the others was made in the meantime, and he stayed put, expecting your father to bring in the command."

He noticed she was weeping, softly and silently. He rose at once, moved to her side and placed his arm around her shoulders. Marcie was having time to think now, and it was hitting hard.

"It'll work out," he said, at a loss for words that had meaning. "It was a terrible shock, but don't let it get too big in your mind, warp the future. . . . Have you relatives somewhere?"

Her head stirred against him. "An uncle—in Pennsylvania."

"Good. That's where you'll go, once we make it to Rolla. I'll put you on the train myself."

"I—I don't know him very well. My mother's brother. . . . He never approved of Father."

"Won't matter. Something like this happens, and the past is forgotten." Jeff straightened, returned to his side of the fire.

Marcie wiped at her eyes with the back of a hand. Glancing at him, she managed a ragged smile. "I'm sorry. It was childish of me to break down."

"Just what you needed."

She took another sip of coffee, made a wry face. "Cold," she said, but refused when he reached for the lard tin. "I was wondering, after what that Confederate lieutenant told us—what will you do with all that money and treasure if the war really is over?"

"It's not," he said flatly. "You can stop believing that."

"But suppose it is—"

"Have to take it back to San Francisco, see that it's returned to the people who did the donating."

"There are some who'd keep it, since nobody would ever know."

"I'm not one of those," he said stiffly, "and I'd sure as hell know."

He saw something break in her eyes, relief possibly, as she set her cup aside. "Will we be near a settlement tomorrow?"

He looked at her suspiciously wondering if there was hidden meaning in the apparently guileless question. After a moment he shrugged.

"Don't know. Country's strange to me. You could even say we're lost except I know we have to keep moving northeast. Going by the sun that's not hard to do."

"Don't you have a map?"

"Went up in smoke along with all my other papers, at Fort Whiterock."

A look of concern crossed her features. "Even your orders?"

"Even those. Got nothing to go on except what I know has to be done."

"But what if Union soldiers stop us?"

"Don't intend to let that happen. They're as dangerous to me and what I'm doing as the Rebs—or the Apaches."

"I don't see why—"

"Well, they are," he replied, unwilling to go into it. Knocking the ash from his pipe, he glanced to the black velvet sky, hung low and strung with glittering stars. "Get some rest," he said, rising. "Long day tomorrow."

She arose, wrapping the blanket closer around her. "Do you think we'll have trouble?"

"I think we'll have that every day—and night too," he said, crossing to the wagon. "Fix your bed in here. I'll stick close to the mules."

Well before sunrise, stiff and cold, they were on their way. The mules, lively after the feeding and a night's rest, trotted easily, taking the grade to the summit with no effort.

They topped out the mountain, going through a natural pass, and looked down upon a broad plain that ended only against a smudge of mountains far to the east. Almost immediately the road forked, one branch leading straight on, the second angling left. That, if it continued its course, led in the proper direction.

Halted, Marshak considered the advisability of taking the less-traveled route. He must continue to bear north, he realized; due east would lead him into Texas and thoroughly hostile country. It was only logical to swing north until he reached the Rio Grande. Once there he'd be in a position to take more accurate bearings.

A distant, hollow thud far back down the mountain jarred him to sudden alert. Gripping the rifle, he dropped from the wagon and returned to the summit, a dozen paces away. Keeping close to the wall of the pass, he looked down-slope.

Three riders, barely distinguishable. Not soldiers, and they didn't appear to be Indians. Jeff remained there, watching intently. Something bright flashed in the sunlight. Silver. . . . A heavily decorated saddle, he concluded. The men could be Mexicans—*vaqueros,* and possibly bandits. They were far from the border, however.

He decided he was unduly alarmed. After all, it was a main road traveled no doubt by many pilgrims passing to and from various points. Simply because it was the same route taken by him did not necessarily indicate those he saw on it were following his tracks.

But the assumption failed to satisfy him. Too much was at stake. He watched for another five minutes, and then, with an unaccountable disquiet gnawing at him, retraced his steps to the wagon. Taking the near mule by the bridle, he moved the rig down the north road for a short distance.

He then doubled back to the split in the trail, and ripping a leafy branch from a clump of scrub oak, thoroughly swept away the prints left by the wagon wheels and the team. When he had finished there was no evidence that anyone had swung off the main route.

Marcie faced him anxiously when he climbed onto the seat and headed the mules on downgrade. "What was it?"

"Three riders. Coming up the trail."

He heard her breath catch. "Following us?"

"Hard to say. Could be drifters, or just somebody going somewhere."

Marshak dropped it there, having no desire to go further into the matter. It wasn't possible, he knew, but one of the men looked like Wade Krause.

16

They saw no more of the three riders, and Jeff guessed they had continued on east. There was no way of knowing their identities, of course, nor was there any reason to believe they had been following Marcie and him. He was simply overcautious, he told himself when they halted for night camp. Likely, as he had assured Marcie, they were only drifters. As for Wade Krause—dead men don't ride horses.

He dismissed the outlaw and the incident from his mind, set about bedding down the all-important mules, again marveling at the condition of the big, hard-bodied brutes. They were thinner than when the journey began, but it was a sleek leanness that lent them a powerful, steel-strong look. He'd keep them that way; good care, rest, water and regular portions of grain to supplement the grass they were able to forage, was the key.

Eventually they would need to be reshod. He wondered how he could manage that since Marcie, and her promise to flee at the first opportunity, made it impossible for him to visit any settlement where a blacksmith would be available. He brushed the problem aside, finally. He'd find a solution when the time came.

Marshak, having thoughts of the girl, paused to watch her moving about the wagon, setting out the articles for the evening meal. His hopes for cooperation on her part had dwindled gradually that day as the hot, dry hours wore on and she lapsed deeper into stubborn silence.

That night before, on the mountain, she had become friendly, companionable, seemingly willing to assist in the task he had undertaken. But that had vanished. Now, again, she was the Marcie he had come to know—obstinate, withdrawn and undoubtedly seeking above all the opportunity for escape.

He pondered the change. Had he said or done something that caused her feeling toward him to alter? Had she given her situation consideration during the night, become more determined than ever to get free of him? In disgust he gave up thinking about it. There was no understanding Marcie Denton, but one thing was certain, she'd still be with him when he got to Rolla—she could bank on it!

The evening meal was a quiet one, and when it was over and the necessary chores done, Marcie climbed into her bed in the wagon with barely a nod. Marshak remained by the fire for a time, smoking and enjoying a last cup of coffee, and then he, too, turned in.

Thus it went for the several days and nights that followed, the monotonous pattern of moving steadily across sometimes broken, other times flat, but always burning land; the night halts wherein the wall of silence that hung between them in daylight thickened and perhaps became more impenetrable with darkness.

Eventually, after bucking a sand-filled wind while they traversed a rough, lava rock-strewn plain frowned upon by five black-capped volcanic cones, they came to the Rio Grande. Marshak was certain of the river's identity; they had forded two or three other streams, all small but this one was wide, sluggish and flowed purposefully within its cottonwood- and willow-lined banks.

He felt better now that they had reached a definite landmark. . . . Follow the Rio upstream to where it curved away from the road, then bear true northeast. That had been the plan. This would take him to Santa Fe and adjacent Fort Marcy, lead him on by the upper boundary of the Texas Panhandle and into the comparative security of Indian Territory.

He'd need to alter his intentions somewhat now. No longer could he risk Santa Fe and Fort Marcy, and if Union forces at Fort Craig, near Mesilla, had failed to halt Confederate Colonel Baylor and his army, the entire Territory could be overrun with gray-clad soldiers. . . . And even if this had not come to pass, he'd have Union patrols to reckon with. Add to all that his problems with Marcie and the possibility of hostile Indians. . . .

Jeff sighed, considering the near futility of it. He'd be glad when it was over—glad when the train rolled into Washington, and he could deliver his charge to the Secretary in the Capitol Building. The California War Chest was becoming a ponderous millstone hanging from his neck; the moment when he would be free of it could not arrive too soon.

They rested along the Rio Grande for an hour, during

which time Marshak took the opportunity of erecting a canopy over the wagon seat, using arched willows and a blanket. It was a crude arrangement but it would serve to keep the sun and rain off them during the balance of the journey, and he wondered why he hadn't thought of it sooner.

They forded the river in midmorning, finding the bed loose with silt but not treacherous, and a short time later halted in a brushy grove a quarter mile from a small town.

Jeff, on edge, had no liking for what must be done; however not only were they running low on provisions but the grain so necessary for the wellbeing of the mules was almost depleted, and in a broad land where human habitation was notable for its rarity, he felt he dare not pass up the occasion.

Climbing down, he uncoiled the rope hooked over the off-mule's collar, snapped one end to the bridle ring, tied the other securely to a sturdy tree. Turning then to the wagon bed he rummaged about until he found a length of cord. Taking it, he resumed his seat next to Marcie.

"Hold out your hands," he directed.

He complied slowly. In a few deft movements he began to bind her wrists together.

"What are you doing?" she demanded, frantically trying to pull away.

He threw one leg across her lap, pinned her to the seat. "Making sure you don't run away while I'm gone."

Fury brightened her eyes, brought tears. "You—you—" she stammered incoherently.

He shrugged, and climbing over her, dropped to the spongy ground. Taking the loose end of the cord, he made a turn around the arched spring beneath the seat, thus restricting her activity, and fastened the end to a cinch ring on the side of the wagon bed.

Marcie was stiff with anger and frustration, so much so her words made no sense. Marshak stood leaning against the hindquarters of one of the mules, watching her twist and strain against her bonds, and then when she had tired, he reached forward, picked up his rifle.

"Don't like this any more than you do—but you can't be trusted."

"Damn you!" she blazed, renewing her struggles. "I'll not let you—"

"Won't be long," he said, and wheeled away. He'd make it quick. He didn't like leaving Marcie there alone and helpless, and he didn't want to lose any more daylight than was absolutely necessary.

The settlement was small, no more than half a dozen houses clustered in the center of several tiny farms. There was but one general store operated apparently by a Sol Weinman. Jeff paused in the doorway to glance up and down the narrow street, and seeing nothing that disturbed him, stepped inside the low-ceilinged building.

Heat trapped within its four walls was a tangible substance accenting the odors of the establishment's wares, mingling them into a not altogether disagreeable conglomeration.

A squat, round-faced man with steel-rimmed spectacles and wearing a black bib apron over his clothing came from behind a counter.

"Yes? What is it for you?"

"Provisions—and a sack of oats for my team," Marshak said, glancing around.

"Good. . . . Good. . . . What kind of provisions?"

"Coffee—ten pounds. Dry beef. Half a dozen boxes of biscuits." He paused, pointed to several round loaves of bread in a glass case. "Take a few of those. . . . Side of bacon." The bacon would turn rancid before it was used up, but it couldn't be helped. Looking over the shelves he added other items—beans, rice, tinned fruit.

Weinman scurried about collecting the articles ordered, adding those mentioned as they came to Jeff's mind. Finally it was done.

"Got a wheelbarrow I can use to cart this stuff to my wagon? Parked it back in the grove."

The merchant said: "Sure. . . . Bill tots up to twelve dollars, forty cents."

Marshak dropped a double-eagle on the counter, picked up his change. Thrusting the loose coins into his pocket, he asked casually, "How's the war coming?"

Weinman closed his cash box with a snap, looked up in surprise. "How is it you don't know?"

Jeff leaned against the counter. "Driving across country—from the west. Haven't seen anybody for weeks."

"The South's soldiers have moved into Mesilla. That's down in the bottom part of the Territory. They say soon there will be a battle for Fort Craig."

That was good news—no Confederates this far north. Marshak nodded. "What about Washington—back in that part of the country?"

Weinman shrugged his plump shoulders. "News I don't get

much. The capital is Santa Fe. Everything happens there. A stagecoach driver told me the South was winning. A big battle at a place called—a strange name."

"Manassas."

The merchant frowned, scratched at his ear. "There is no news since." Stepping back a few paces, he trundled an often-repaired wheelbarrow into the aisle, positioned it in front of the counter.

"The war from here is a long way. I take no sides. No matter who is winner, it is I still must work for my living. . . . You will bring back the barrow?"

Marshak said, "Sure. . . . How far to Santa Fe?"

"Sixty miles."

"Best road along the river?" Jeff asked, transferring his purchases to the vehicle.

"The mesa road is better. First there is a climb, then it is not so bad. You'll return the wheelbarrow?"

Jeff grinned. "You got my word," he said.

Turning, he moved off through the barrels and boxes scattered about on the floor, and came into the open. The street was still empty and he cut back hurriedly along Weinman's building and entered the field.

Halfway across he paused to wipe sweat from his eyes. Heat was intense in the narrow little valley despite the nearness of a towering mountain range to the east. He'd be glad when he was back in the trees. The shade would feel good and he wished it were possible to make camp where they'd halted, but that was out of the question; there were still several hours of light remaining before darkness set in.

He started forward, halted again, brought up short by the restless stamp of a horse. Releasing the worn handles of the wheelbarrow, he grabbed his rifle, waited, rigid and totally alarmed by the sound. It had not been one of his mules; he had halted the wagon farther to the right, where the trees were more numerous. This had come from the tall brush to his left.

The sound did not come again, and for a brief moment he was tempted to dismiss it as imagination, or at most a straying horse wandering through the grove. But he could not leave it that way—unsettled. Rifle ready, he moved forward, eyes probing the thick growth, ears alert for any unnatural noise.

Three horses. . . .

Marshak dropped low, apprehension building within him. The animals were alone, completely geared, with their reins wound carelessly about the base of a weed clump. Jeff worked in nearer. One of the saddles was an oversized horn rigging, heavy with silver decorations. . . . Mexican. . . . That fact rang a bell deep in his memory. . . . Back on the mountain. . . . A bright flash in the sunlight. He glanced at the animal farthest from him. It wore a U.S. Army brand.

The full implication of that struck him solidly. Wade Krause! He hadn't killed the deserter after all. The man was alive, had evidently recruited partners either in that Mexican village or somewhere along the way, and was again after the gold. His hunch about the three riders had been correct; they were tracking him. He'd thrown them off at the fork, but not for long.

Grim, he moved in, freed the horses, and taking the reins, led them into the brush. Then, using his hat, he sent them trotting off into the distance.

Immediately he doubled back, circling wide, and came to the wagon from the side opposite the settlement. The outlaws would be expecting him to appear from that point. Gaining a stand in the thick shrubbery, he dropped to his knees and worked in close.

Krause, partly hidden, his left arm wound in a dirty bandage, lounged beside the wagon. He was looking up at Marcie, still lashed to the seat spring but now with a gag drawn tight across her lips. A Mexican in *vaquero* trappings was stationed behind one of the larger trees. A third man, wearing range clothing and sporting two ornate holsters complete with pearl-handled pistols, hunched behind a stump to the right of Krause.

Checking the load in his rifle, Marshak rose suddenly to full height. The Mexican saw him first, instantly shouted a warning, and whirled. Jeff fired as the *vaquero* sought safety on the opposite side of the thick-trunked cottonwood, saw bark splinter as the bullet missed. Levering the Henry fast, he shot from the waist at the man with two guns, spinning to bring his weapons into play.

The rifle's heavy slug smashed into the gunman, drove him to the ground. Krause, using the nervously dancing mules as a shield, hunched, triggered his weapon from under the team. The bullet clipped through the brush dangerously close. Jeff leaped to one side, seeking a clear target. He got a fleeting glimpse of the deserter plunging into the brush beyond the wagon. A dozen strides ahead of him was the *vaquero*. Marshak brought his rifle up fast, hesitated as both men disappeared.

Weapon ready for instant use, he raced after the pair, muttering curses at his own ineptitude. He'd let Krause escape again—escape to dog his trail and again make a try for the War Chest. He halted, listened. He could no longer hear the men fleeing through the brush; it would be useless, and foolhardy, to try and hunt them down.

Wise thing would be to return to the wagon, get clear of the valley as fast as possible. Krause and the *vaquero* would lose time rounding up their horses, and there was a good chance he could shake them.

Pivoting, he started back, swung aside when he saw the wheelbarrow standing where he had abandoned it. Grasping the handles, he trotted to the wagon, tossed the load into the bed. Then, releasing the mules, he sprang to the seat, and ignoring Marcie's muffled cries, whipped the team into a hard run.

There wouldn't be time to return Sol Weinman's wheelbarrow, after all.

17

They broke from the field onto a dusty, seldom-used road, no more than dual ruts carved deep in the dark soil. But it took an easterly direction pointing for the upper end of the soaring mountains, and without hesitation Marshak swung the mules onto it.

One thought was uppermost in his mind; Krause and the Mexican had escaped him—he could only try to gain a long lead, lose them again. They'd follow, he knew, but with luck the advantage would be his.

The trail climbed out of the valley, slicing its way through a welter of sandy foothills, leveling finally on a high plain studded with scrub cedars, Spanish bayonet and irregular patches of brush. As the wagon lurched over the last gravelly ridge, Marshak looked back; there was no sign of Krause and his partner.

Tension eased, he turned to Marcie. Her eyes were bright

above the rag tied across her lips, and her hair, free of the sunbonnet, was a tangled, silken mass blowing in the breeze. Wedging the reins between his knees, he released the gag.

"Never figured on Krause," he said with a shake of his head.

Instantly she burst into tears, began jerking at the cord restraining her wrists. Leaning over quickly he began to pull at the knot but could make no progress against the pressure she was exerting on the strands. Her sobs had risen to a scream and he realized that she was hysterical, that the incident in the grove had wholly unnerved her.

Glancing again over his shoulder and seeing there still was no pursuit, he drew the mules to a stop. Then, using both hands, he worked the knot open. In that same fragment of time Marcie leaped from the wagon. Striking hard, she went to her knees, the shrillness of her cries evoking a series of weird echoes.

She was up instantly, running blindly. Startled and momentarily frozen, Jeff sprang from the seat, gave chase. In a dozen strides he caught up. Seizing her by the arm, he spun her about, nerves recoiling at her piercing shrieks. He brought his hand up, slapped her twice across the face. Immediately her body went lax and she wilted against him while low, muffled sobs continued to issue from her throat.

Awkward, he sought to calm her, running his hand over her head, through her hair, patting her gently on the shoulders.

"No need to cry. . . . It's all over."

"Those men—" she murmured. "Those terrible men. . . . The things they said—were going to do. . . . And I couldn't run—do anything. . . ."

Marshak looked toward the valley again, and new fires banked the hatred he held for Wade Krause. "They'll not bother you again," he said. "I'll see to that."

Her sobbing subsided and finally she drew away from him, dabbing at her eyes. "Can we stay here for a little while—just rest?"

Urgency was back with him again, pressing, goading, allowing him no surcease. "Already lost more than an hour. And we'd best keep moving. . . . You'll be all right."

She flung him a baffled, furious look, spun and returned to the wagon. He followed quickly, reached her as she began to climb the wheel spokes, helped her onto the seat. Then, crawling over, he took up the reins and clucked the mules into a trot.

Marcie was forgetting that Krause and the *vaquero* would be following, that his desire to cover as much ground as possible each day was not the only reason for denying her request. She should realize that, but Jeff Marshak was in no mood to make her aware of the fact.

Several times during the succeeding hours he glanced back but could see no riders on the horizon. He was not reassured; Krause and the Mexican were there somewhere, were simply taking pains to keep out of sight until opportunity presented itself. He would have felt better could he have seen them.

They made camp that night well after dark at the foot of a steep bluff and a considerable distance off the road. Odds were better than good, Jeff reasoned, the outlaws would make another attempt soon and he selected their site with an eye to defense.

"No fire," he said, pausing at his chores. "Glare would be seen for miles, bring them right to us."

Marcie, glum the entire day, seemed now to be in better spirits. She smiled, was almost gay when she made her reply.

"I understand. I'll fix something that won't need cooking."

Jeff stared at her suspiciously, unable to comprehend another reversal in her attitude. He had expected her to sulk; instead she was cooperative, verged on the edge of being happy. Sighing, he turned to completing one of the innumerable minor repairs that continually cropped up in the wagon's running gear. There was no understanding Marcie Denton. . . . Again he hesitated, and a bleak smile tugged at his lips. Maybe he understood her after all.

The evening meal was done with quickly, both missing the solace of hot coffee. Marcie crawled into her bed as soon as the dishes were dispatched and Marshak, refilling the magazine of the Henry rifle, and taking a blanket, climbed to a ledge in the bluff where he could look back over the land across which they had traveled.

The moon was dying and only the stars paled the slopes and flats, softening the harsh contours, covering all with a false gentleness. It was a vast, raw world, he acknowledged, but a fine one, and someday he'd like to come again, have time to look, to get the feel—

His brooding contemplation ceased. Far to the west the glow of a campfire laid its yellow-orange mark against the night. A large fire, to be so distinguishable, and placed somewhere near the road.

Krause? It seemed unlikely the deserter and his Mexican

ally would advertise their presence so boldly, being fully aware that he expected them. It could be a ruse, one calculated to lull him into security, hold his attention while they slipped forward in the darkness.

That appeared to be the fact. The fire never dwindled, as one left unattended would naturally do; from time to time it seemed to grow brighter, clear evidence that fuel was being added periodically.

Another party? Possibly, but he had seen no signs of anyone on the mesa—unless, of course, they had moved in from the side late in the day. There should have been dust, however.

Marshak gave up speculation, settled down to a lonely vigil. He was tired and dozed fitfully, but his built-in mechanism of watchfulness never permitted him to sleep for long. And each time he wakened, the fire was there, its stain bright in the distance.

Morning came finally, cold and with a sky banked by dark-bellied, gray clouds. Jeff surveyed them with misgivings; a rain flooding the deep arroyos, making crossings difficult and softening the mountain clay soil on the slopes to sticky, encumbering mud, was something he didn't need. Stiff, ill-humored, he made his way down to the wagon.

Surprisingly, Marcie was up, already preparing a breakfast. She greeted him with a smile, nodded at the fire.

"I thought it would be all right. Was careful to use dry wood."

He mumbled assent, put himself to the task of readying the mules for the day. When he was finished Marcie had food waiting, and in less than an hour after rising, they were on the road. Working together they had accomplished it all in record time.

Marshak wished it could be that way in the days to come, but he held little hope. He had come to know Marcie Denton in their many weeks of association, and while in such a cooperative state she was suspect. There was reason behind it, he was convinced—but she'd not fool him.

"I'm glad there was no trouble last night," she said, adjusting the flapping edge of the makeshift canopy above her head. "You needed sleep. Caught you dozing several times before we stopped."

He hadn't gotten much rest but he made no mention of the fact.

She twisted about, laid her arm upon the back-rest of the

seat. "I don't see Krause and that other man anywhere. Maybe they've given up. Your shooting their friend—"

"Won't stop Krause."

"How can you be sure? If they meant to try again wouldn't they have done it last night?"

He moved his shoulders. "There was a fire back on the flats. Don't know whether it was them or not. Was somebody."

Marcie fell silent, considered that. After a time she sighed. "He won't ever give up, will he? He'll keep trying until you kill him—or he kills you."

"Expect that's the way it'll end."

Rain, fortunately, failed to materialize during the day, and late in the afternoon, after a cool journey during which they had covered far more miles than Jeff had hoped for, they pulled into a shallow draw for the night. An ominous cracking had developed in the right rear wheel of the wagon, and he wanted daylight to make an inspection, and repair, if possible.

There had been no indication that Krause and the *vaquero* were in the vicinity, but again Marshak took precautions. They omitted a fire, and when the meal was over, he stationed himself a short distance from camp where he could watch the road and the land surrounding.

It had been a pleasant day, for Marcie Denton's mood had not changed. She had remained talkative and agreeable and that next morning when they swung onto the road, he began to wonder if perhaps he were misjudging her.

Could it be she had come around to his way of thinking, was willing now to work with rather than obstinately oppose everything he deemed necessary and important? It would be a fine thing if it were so. Many tiresome miles lay ahead for them. The drudgery of the hours would pass much more quickly if she—

Marshak saw the Union Army patrol in that moment, whirled the wagon off the road instantly into a brush-filled arroyo.

Understanding came to him in that same instant. The campfire had been that of the cavalrymen. Their presence also explained why Krause had made no move, had elected instead to wait for a more opportune time when there'd be no possibility of interference.

And Marcie. . . . His lips curled as realization dawned. She'd seen them that previous day, too, and made no mention of it.

18

"Help!"

Marcie Denton's cry shattered the thoughts racing through Marshak's mind. He spun to the girl, grabbed frantically to prevent her leaping from the wagon, missed.

"Here—over here!"

The cavalrymen were too far away to hear, but if she got beyond the arroyo, started running across the flat toward them, one was certain to notice.

He was after her like a tall, silent cat, throwing himself from the seat, landing lightly, and streaking across the loose rock and weedy growth in pursuit. He caught her just as she reached the opposite slope of the dry wash, dragged her down.

"Shut up!" he snarled, clapping a hand over her mouth.

She fought him like a tigress, hammering at his bearded face with small fists, kicking at his legs.

"Let me go!" she cried, twisting her head to one side. "Let me go!"

He stifled her words again, held her locked to him in a crushing embrace. Breathing hard, she began to weaken, and then accepting the fruitlessness of her efforts, lay quiet.

Jeff, not trusting her at all, maintained his grip upon her body, raised himself slightly until he could see over the rim of the arroyo. . . . A dozen or so men and one officer. . . . Three loaded pack animals. . . . Headed southeast. From Fort Marcy, or possibly Union, out to keep an eye on the Texas border. Sighing, he sank back. It had been a close thing.

He looked at Marcie. She was flushed but breathing normally again, now watched him with a steady hate glowing in her wide-set eyes.

"I'll get away next time," she said, firm promise in her voice. "Wait and see."

"Be no next time," he said. "You'll not get the chance."

Her smile was forced. "You can't watch me every moment—I've told you that."

"I can tie and gag you. . . . Maybe you like that."

Involuntarily she shuddered, turned away with a helpless gesture. "Why couldn't we have joined those soldiers? They were Union. They could have helped us."

"You know the answer to that," he snapped.

"That court-martial? I don't believe you. Papers on that are at Fort Craig—hundreds of miles from here. Nobody up here knows a thing about it."

"Probably right. Only copies would be in Washington. But that isn't it. How would I explain the Army property I'm using? I've got no orders to show, nothing to prove what I'd tell them."

"They wouldn't shoot you for that. All they'd do would be to take you back to wherever they're from—Fort Marcy probably. And once you were there you could insist they get in touch with Washington."

"Way things stand, it would take weeks. I'd sit there and rot while some desk-brass fumbled around in his spare time trying to get to the bottom of it—you've got to remember only a very few know about this mission. And by the time the matter was straightened out, secrecy would be lost, and everything would be in the open—including those damned court-martial charges. Probably end up with somebody else completing the job."

"That's really what bothers you most, isn't it!" she flared, eyes blazing. "This—this completing your mission! It's all that means anything to you—not me, not even yourself—only getting the job done! Is it so important because you're a—a foreigner? Is that why you'll do anything to get through?"

Foreigner. . . . Jeff Marshak had a quick recollection of many times behind barracks and stables where he'd used his fists to rectify that implied designation of inferiority. . . . And after he had become an officer, the quiet but equally bloody affairs to accomplish the same purpose. . . . All that had been a matter of personal satisfaction. This was something else—at least it seemed so to him.

"Guess every man has to prove himself one way or another," he said. "Had my share doing just that. This is different. I'm not trying to prove anything. They handed me a job to do—an important one. I aim to do it."

"Not it at all," she said stubbornly. "I've been around the Army all my life. I never heard of a man so dedicated, so determined to carry out an order regardless of cost. It isn't natural—normal."

He thought of Jeremiah Denton and the kind of soldier he was; a scathing retort leaped quickly to his lips, but he let it die, finding he had no desire to be cruel to her despite the way she felt about him.

"Matter of values, I suppose," he said, rising. "We all look at things in a different light."

The patrol was gone, lost behind a lengthy roll of land separating two distant hill formations. "Best we move on," he said, extending his hand.

She ignored the offer, rose to her feet. Her cheeks were bright and the same glow filled her eyes. "If you're implying that my father—"

"Implying nothing," he said wearily. "What's so wrong with a soldier carrying out an order from a superior? Where's the sin in that?"

"Nothing's wrong with it, but orders are carried out within reason. It doesn't become a fixation—a madness that wipes out everything human and decent. It's not supposed to turn a man into some kind of cold-blooded animal!"

Marshak stared at her, taken aback by the fury of her words. And then he laughed. "Animal! A crazy, foaming-at-the-mouth animal! Guess, with this beard and my hair down to my shoulders, I look the part. But, lady, I assure you I'm far from that—I'm sane as you."

Reaching out, he swung her off her feet, and carrying her easily as he would a child, crossed to the wagon and deposited her solidly on the seat. She was too startled to make any outcry, simply waited in frightened silence while he climbed up beside her, backed the rig around and once again was on the road.

He was grateful for her bitter silence. He needed to think. Likely there would be other soldiers patrolling the area, since the commanders at Marcy and Union would maintain close surveillance on the Texas border. To that danger must be added the continuing threat of Wade Krause and the *vaquero.*

From those two he could expect an all-out attempt, sooner or later, to obtain the War Chest. It would be different where soldiers were concerned. They would simply take him captive, and as he had explained to Marcie, interrupt and cancel out all plans for the mission. He stirred restlessly. The future wasn't promising—not with death on one hand, total personal failure on the other.

He left a decoy fire that night for Krause and his companion. Building it off the road in a secluded pocket of hills where it was evident but not obvious, he laid the wood so that the fire would be self-feeding for several hours.

Then, breaking the usual nightfall pattern, he continued on, taking advantage of the knowledge that Krause, spotting the glow from the flames, would employ care and use a maximum of time to work in close. It gave him satisfaction to think he would thus increase the distance between the outlaws and himself by many miles before the ruse was discovered—if it worked.

Evidently it did. In the days following, they progressed without incident, seeing nothing of the deserter and fortunately, no more soldiers. They lost a full twelve hours in a remote village where Marshak had the mules reshod, using the shoes he carried as extras, while he repaired the wheel that had given him cause for worry.

Marcie behaved very well, possibly because there could be nothing gained by breaking away in so small and desolate a settlement, anyway, and soon they were again moving on, apparently no worse off for the delay.

As more time passed, nothing changed between Marcie and Jeff Marshak. They lived, worked and rode together in a sort of soundless vacuum where words were passed from one to the other from necessity only. Many times he endeavored to draw her out as the monotonous days dragged by, but her reaction was negative, her replies brief and reflected no interest.

Eventually he gave it up entirely. Let her have it that way, if she wished. Rolla was emerging slowly now as a reality and not, as in the beginning, no more than a name on a map.

19

They had reached the Indian Territory.

That conviction grew within Jeff Marshak as they worked gradually off a high plateau of sweeping, grassy swales and entered a rough land of many buttes. Then, late one afternoon when they reached a fairly wide river of little water flowing quietly over a bed of white sand, he knew; they were on the Cimarron.

He could take a different bearing now. Missouri lay to the east, hundreds of miles distant, to be sure, but at least he could plan a definite route and not travel only in a general direction.

Marcie, unmoving on the seat while the mules waded out fetlock-deep to slake their thirst, finally turned to him. There was a pleading note in her voice.

"Can we take time for a bath—please? It's been so long. . . ."

He stared at her, grinned. All those blind, uncertain miles of constant danger across New Mexico and when they do arrive at a point where they definitely know their position—the first thing she thinks of is a bath!

He stood up, looked back over the course they had followed. No riders were in sight. Krause and the Mexican could have taken a wrong trail when he and Marcie had halted at that village for repairs. It was a warming thought.

He swung his gaze full circle, remembering where they were. . . . Indian country—unpredictable Indians, he'd been warned. There were those considered friendly, other tribes outright hostile. . . . A new danger to bear in mind. But he saw only the starkly beautiful land lying hushed under a cooling sun.

"All right," he said. "Got some harness that needs mending. Tend to that while you're having your bath."

Marcie expressed her thanks with a silent nod. Climbing down from the wagon she walked to the edge of the stream, glanced along the low bank uncertainly. There were no sheltered coves, no overhanging brush. He understood her dilemma.

"I'll pull back a ways," he said.

Swinging the mules about, he drove for a distance of fifty yards or so and halted. When he looked toward her again, she was lost to view.

Marcie returned before he had finished his chore and he paused to give her an appreciating glance. The bathing had done much for her; she appeared fresh, rested and in better spirits. She had made use of the opportunity to wash her dress and wring it dry. It was bleached now and showed signs of constant wear.

"Do we follow the river?" she asked, sitting near the wagon and starting to braid her dark hair.

"No," Jeff replied, resuming his work. "Way I remember that map, the Cimarron turns north. We go due east."

She sighed. "The bath was nice."

"There'll be other rivers. Lots of them from here on."

She seemed to realize suddenly where they were. "This is bad country, isn't it? Indians, I mean."

It was good to have her carrying on a conversation again. He shrugged. "Had Apaches all across New Mexico, along with our friend Krause."

She arched her brows. "There's been no sign of him. Maybe he's given up."

"No such good luck. Might have lost our trail, but he and his Mexican *compadre* won't quit. Been thinking they may have changed their plan, swung around and got in front of us. Krause knows we're headed for Rolla."

She lapsed into silence and Marshak cursed himself for having mentioned the probability. She had emerged from her shell, likely now he had given her cause to retreat once more, and worry.

"Something else," he said. "Think our best bet will be to travel nights, hole up in the daylight. Less chance of trouble."

She nodded disinterestedly. "How long will it take to reach Missouri?"

"Ten, maybe twelve days."

Marcie sighed, studied her hands, now folded in her lap. "Seems like it's been years. I'll be glad when it's over—if ever it is."

"We'll make it," Marshak said quietly.

They left the Cimarron late that evening, and for the next two nights traversed fairly level country, making good time. Marshak employed a simple method for maintaining his easterly route; at each sundown he would determine exact east from his shadow, and select some distant landmark of prominence and point for it. With darkness it often became indistinguishable, of course; but his own reliable sense of direction once enjoined, guided him unvaryingly and they strayed but little from the line chosen until the first streaks of dawn appeared, when any necessary corrections could be made.

They crossed the Cimarron again four nights later, finding it much deeper and running swift. They were not far south of Kansas, he realized, had in fact been moving along its border for some time. He derived an odd sort of satisfaction from the knowledge that they were near a state, even one of so recent vintage, rather than a territory. Somehow it made him feel civilization was closer.

He had, during the planning of the journey, considered entering Kansas once he'd made it to Indian Territory. There was word that the Kansas-Pacific Railway Company was extending its lines, and a rail-head would thus be nearer than Rolla.

But he could get no confirmation and abandoned the idea. Besides, Kansas, involved in what virtually amounted to a private war with Missouri and plagued by guerrilla bands, was no place to be transporting a fortune in gold and precious gems.

They forded the Arkansas near daylight two mornings after they'd put the Cimarron behind them, encountering no serious problems other than the reluctance of the mules to tread in deep water. Soon they were in salt-plains country and Marshak, finding no camping site suitable, drove later than usual, halting finally in a small stand of trees clustered along a creek.

They spent the day there, going through the necessary procedures that had long since become routine, slept, and when the shadows began to lengthen, prepared to leave. Jeff, hunched over, arranging the blanket at their feet, caught motion to his right from the tail of an eye.

"Indians!" Marcie gasped in that same instant.

Marshak's jaw settled into a hard line. They'd been lucky. Better than halfway across the undisputed domain of the redmen and these were the first they had encountered. Making no outward indication that he had even noticed the braves, he put the mules into movement.

A dozen warriors. . . . They looked different from the Apache, wore more clothing and feathers; a considerable amount of red and yellow paint streaked their dark faces and arms. They rode sleek ponies, held them at a distance of a hundred yards or so while they maintained pace with the mules. Jeff looked close, tried to see if they were armed with rifles. He thought he spotted one or two but couldn't be sure in the failing light.

"What can we do?"

There was a tremor in Marcie's voice and he knew that since the horror she had experienced at Whiterock, the sight of Indians would forever evoke strong fear within her.

"Nothing," he said. "We'll just keep moving. Could be they're only curious."

She was staring at the riders with a sort of rapt fascination. "They look so strong—proud."

And bloodthirsty, he thought but did not put into words. He had learned to keep the brutal facts to himself. It was not the same, being with a woman all of the time, instead of a man. He'd discovered that bald truth was not always wise.

"Don't think they intend to bother us," he said after they had continued on through the growing moonlight for a considerable distance. "They'll pull off when they've got their fill of looking."

But when sunrise came after a night of tension, the Indians were still there, silently keeping abreast at their chosen distance.

Marshak stopped that morning on a low hill, made camp where protection in the form of dense brush was the only thing available, and spent a nervous day under the watchful eyes of the warriors. When they moved on at darkness, the Indians moved also and another tense night began.

By midnight Jeff Marshak had reached the point where he almost wished they would attack, if such was their intention; his nerves, as well as Marcie's, were at the breaking point. And then, with morning, patience evaporated. Temper sharp, he drew the team to a halt. He could stand it no longer—and Marcie was bordering on hysterics.

She turned to him at once, ashen from the strain. "What is it? Why are you stopping so early?"

"Damned if we're going through any more of this," he said harshly, picking up his rifle.

She flinched, alarmed. "You're not going to try to fight them. . . . So many—"

Jeff shook his head, dropped to the ground. "Aim to give them a look at something they've never seen—a repeater rifle in action. Maybe it'll help them make up their minds if they figure on moving in."

He walked a short distance from the wagon toward the Indians, milling about in a tight group, watching him intently. Pausing, Marshak glanced around, settled his eyes on a large, white-faced rock some fifty yards to the left of the braves.

Holding the rifle over his head so they could see clearly what it was, he lowered it into place, took aim and poured fifteen bullets into the rock as rapidly as he could lever the Henry's mechanism.

The effect was magical. Amid the rolling chain of echoes, several excited yells went up from the warriors. The group became more agitated, began wheeling back and forth, pointing and shouting. The display had unquestionably astounded and frightened them; a weapon that hurled an endless stream of bullets without being reloaded. It was beyond understanding.

Tall and rigid before the braves, Marshak held his position for a long minute and then wheeling, returned to the wagon and resumed his seat. Picking up the reins, he reached into his pocket for a handful of cartridges.

"Reload it," he said, dropping the shells into her lap and clucking the mules forward.

She was hesitant. Without looking he showed her how to insert the brass loads into the slot on the underside of the tubular magazine. Marcie caught on instantly.

"What are they doing?" he asked, keeping his eyes straight ahead.

"Haven't moved, hardly. A couple of them are looking at the rock."

A few minutes later all had disappeared, vanishing into the rolling hills as abruptly as they had come. The demonstration of the Henry's firepower had done the trick.

Marcie breathed a sigh of thankfulness. "I was so frightened," she said, unconsciously laying her hand on his arm. "If you hadn't thought to—" She checked herself, abruptly aware of the display of familiarity, and pulled back.

"Remembered how the Apaches acted when they first saw it used," he said. "Was hoping it would work again. Was even better."

"You think they'll follow us?"

Jeff shook his head. "Doubt it."

He was right. They halted shortly after that in a shaded area near a small stream, for camp, and while he was certain in mind they'd seen the last of the braves, he nevertheless kept watch throughout the day, sleeping only in fitful snatches. When sundown came and they were ready to move on, no Indians were in sight.

Marshak was becoming more convinced, as time wore on, that Krause and the *vaquero* were now somewhere in front of him, and he became more sharply alert for evidence of the pair.

The country through which they were passing was thickly wooded in places, with many hills between which the wagon was compelled to pass. It was ideal for ambush. But as more time elapsed and there was no attempt, new thoughts entered his mind; perhaps the outlaws had gotten themselves thoroughly lost—or possibly they had run into trouble with Indians.

He wished he knew for certain—it was the not knowing that troubled him. But now a worry of a different sort had returned to haunt him. They were again running low on supplies—food for Marcie and himself, the all-important grain for the mules. He'd have to find a settlement soon.

The answer came much quicker than expected. Early one morning, as they moved slowly up a long grade cleaving two hills of more than usual height, they broke out onto a small flat and looked into a broad valley. Smoke and the roofs of a small settlement were immediately visible.

"A town!" Marcie cried, quickly aroused. "What is it?"

Jeff frowned, having no idea. "Don't remember the map of this part."

The mules, as if sensing relief, began to trot on the downgrade, and just as the sun broke over the eastern horizon, they reached the outskirts of the village. A man, walking along the edge of the road, hoe across his shoulder, paused as they drew abreast.

"Morning," he greeted.

Marshak nodded. "A fine one. What town is this?"

The farmer lowered the hoe, leaned on it. "Willow Grove."

Jeff thought back, struggled to remember. He could revive no recollection of the name "Willow Grove," he repeated. "Willow Grove what?"

The man turned his head to the side, spat tobacco juice at a fence post. "Reckon you all are strangers for sure. Willow Grove, Missouri—that's what."

20

Missouri!

Marshak was at once elated and disturbed. Rolla was near now, a glowing, golden gate that led to safety and the end of a tedious, nerve-wracking trail.

But it foretold other, new problems. He would need to watch Marcie more closely, for his need for her would be even greater. They would encounter many persons, undoubtedly a large number of soldiers—and that multipled the risk of using Army property. He needed new, reasonable explanations for the questions that were certain to be asked.

"Where you folks from?" the farmer asked, sauntering forward.

Jeff motioned toward the north. "Back up that way a piece."

The man was silent, eyes on the coffin. "Been some sadness in your family?"

"Brother," Marshak replied, grasping an opportunity. "Taking him to Rolla for burial."

"Rolla? Well, I declare. Got some relations up there myself. Name of Gebhardt—same as mine. Cousins, however."

"May get a chance to look them up. This the best way to go?"

"Sure is. Just keep going right on through town till you pass the schoolhouse, then take the turn to the left. Runs smackdab into Rolla."

"Good road?"

"Plenty good. Usually lots of folks traveling that way. Railroad's there. Somebody coming or going all the time."

It wasn't what Jeff Marshak wanted to hear; a well-used highway meant trouble. He'd look for an alternate route that paralleled, one that came in for less traffic.

"Shouldn't take long to get there then," he said.

"No more'n a couple of days," Gebhardt said. "Less'n that if you keep them mules moving."

Rolla. . . . Within two days reach. . . . It was hard to make himself believe it. He grinned at the farmer. "Sure been a pleasure talking to you," he said, and started the team.

"Same here," Gebhardt answered. "Good luck."

There were other questions Marshak would have liked to ask but they could wait until later—until he was in the town. The problem of how best to manage that arose in his mind. He glanced at Marcie.

"Have to stop here. Don't like the idea but it has to be done. Several things we need."

She nodded, face tilted slightly upward as she looked toward the village.

"Figure to leave the wagon somewhere at the edge of town where it won't draw attention, walk in. Can do this two ways. You can stay on the seat, tied down like before, or—"

He paused, watched her stiffen as the remembrance of that came to her. She did not turn, kept her eyes forward.

"Or?"

"You can walk in with me, at my side, hanging to my arm like a wife would. You won't open your mouth, leave the talking to me."

She faced him frankly. "What if I did, and then called for help. Would you use that?" She pointed to the rifle propped against this knee.

"After getting this far I'm not likely to let you or anyone else stop me now," he said quietly.

She had no immediate answer for that, and then finally: "I'll go with you. Be good to walk in a street again, see people—stores, even houses."

Marshak waited for the rest of it.

"You have my promise. I'll be no trouble."

"Good," he said, relieved. He had not relished the thought of binding her, leaving her helpless and alone again. "We'll find a spot somewhere along here, hide the rig. Wish I could trade off the mules. Bound to be plenty of army around."

"The mud you rubbed on worked fine."

"For just a glance, maybe. But if some smart jasper took a notion to look close—"

A tall, two-storied rock structure loomed up on their right as they rounded a bend. An abandoned mill, apparently. Unhesitating, Marshak pointed for it, drove the mules in behind. The sound of a fast-running creek greeted them from the shadows as he brought the team to a halt.

"Water and grass," he murmured, climbing down and reaching for Marcie. "Couldn't be better."

He swung her lightly to the ground, turned to make the mules comfortable during their absence. Then, taking his rifle he moved with Marcie back to the road. They'd make an incongruous pair—he with his long hair, beard, tattered clothing and rifle, she in a faded dress and sunbonnet many times her size.

They reached the end of the street and stopped. Stores lined both sides for a short distance; behind those were the residences, tall, narrow frame houses with pitched roofs and, almost without variation, painted white. Flowers and huge trees—walnut, maple and elm, grew in every yard and each supported a flourishing vegetable garden.

"Like a picture," Marcie murmured, enthralled by her first look in months at civilization.

Marshak's sharp glance was roving the street in hurried survey. There were few persons abroad, the hour being early. He was relieved to see no blue uniforms, or gray either, for that matter. Bringing his attention back, he started a second probe, searching now for a general store.

The Willow Grove Hotel. . . . The Willow Grove Café. . . . Willow Grove Christian Church. . . . Jeff had a better understanding of the farmer's indignation; it would be difficult not to know the name of the settlement. Tugging at Marcie's arm, he moved on, angling toward Zurcher's mercantile establishment on the opposite side of the street.

En route they encountered two or three individuals, none of whom paid them more than ordinary attention, seeming intent instead upon serious business of their own. The war caused that—made a man think of other things.

The war. . . .

Marshak wondered how it was going. What had occurred in Washington after that disastrous clash at—at—he fumbled for the name—Manassas? Much could have transpired since then. Had the Confederacy pushed on, victorious in its march? Or had the Union squared itself and driven back the Rebels? It seemed strange wondering about something that involved his own country so vitally, and him, personally. Well, he'd soon know.

They stepped up onto the broad porch of the general store, crossed to the entrance and moved inside. Jeff halted, hearing Marcie sigh contentedly at the jumbled scene before her. She was like a person of deep emotional nature beholding something of great beauty for the first time.

"Morning, folks," a lean, stooped man with an iron-gray trailing moustache arose from a rocking chair in a back corner. Setting aside the curved stem pipe he held, he shuffled to a point behind a short counter. "What'll it be?"

"Coffee," Marshak began, and hurriedly went through a list of needed items, concluding with, "Oats, if you've got some."

"Sure," Zurcher said, studying Jeff thoughtfully. "That coffee, you want it ground?"

Marshak nodded. A tenseness was gripping him. He felt ill-at-ease under the sharp, watchful eyes of the storekeeper. There was something in the man's manner that disturbed him. He glanced at Marcie, leisurely drifting among the merchandise displays, turned back to Zurcher.

"How's the war going?"

The storekeeper paused in the process of assembling the order. "So-so. Ain't much fighting going, excepting amongst ourselves. President's hollering for more soldiers—forty, fifty thousand. . . . You folks must be living mighty far back in the hills if you ain't heard nothing about it."

"Been out of touch," Marshak said. "Last I heard there'd been a fight somewhere close to Washington. Manassas, I think."

Zurcher's movements became studied and deliberate.

"Was told the Union took a licking there."

"Maybe so. Didn't do them Secesh no good. Never got to Washington." Zurcher looked up slyly. "Where'd you say you hailed from?"

"Didn't say, but we're from west of here."

"Around Indian Territory, that it?"

"Close."

Jeff pointed to a bolt of cheesecloth on a shelf to the right of the storekeeper, an idea coming to him. "Give me about six yards of that."

Zurcher bobbed his head, measured off the specified amount, folded it and handed it to Marshak who thrust it into his pocket.

"Oats—that what you said?"

"Half a sack," Jeff answered.

The store owner came from behind the counter, turned toward a door at the rear of the room. "Be a minute or two while I get some," he said.

Marshak glanced questioningly at the sacks of feed stacked neatly against the wall at the end of the counter. Alarm and suspicion rocked through him. Moving quickly, he stepped beyond the counter, crossed to the doorway into which Zurcher had disappeared, halted. The storekeeper's guarded voice came to him.

". . . and get them up here in a hurry. Tell the Major it's more of them Secesh trash. Hear what he called Bull Run? Manassas. That's what the Secesh calls it. I'll stall them long as I can but—"

Marshak waited to hear no more. Wheeling, he strode to Marcie, seized her by the arm and hustled her out onto the porch.

"What—" she began in mild protest.

"That storekeeper—Zurcher. Thinks we're Confederates. Sending somebody for the Army."

They reached the walk, veered into the street toward the old mill. A man standing at the corner gave them a puzzled look as they hurried by, wondering no doubt at their haste rather than their outlandish appearance.

Reaching the end of the street Marshak glanced over his shoulder. Zurcher and a short, heavy woman were out in front of the store. The storekeeper was waving his arms, shouting at someone farther down, hidden from Jeff's view.

"Run," he said tensely, and broke into a trot.

21

They reached the wagon, Marshak thankful he had not taken time to remove the mule's harness. Marcie climbed onto the seat as he freed the tether rope, and holding to the near mule's bridle, turned the team around. Then, leaping to the girl's side, he cut across the narrow strip of ground to the road.

He paused. The way to Rolla lay at the opposite end of Willow Grove. Taking the usual route down the main street was out of the question now. . . . There had to be another road or street other than the one fronting the stores. Steep hills lay to the right of the settlement, a gradual sloping away to its left. If there were a secondary route it would have to lie in that direction.

Immediately he put the mules into motion, slashing across the highway at right angles, dipping down at once into a narrow, grass-filled gully. The wagon rocked and bounced and the mules, sliding, began to hold back in the harness as the grade steepened. Keeping a tight rein, Jeff stood upright, eyes probing the shadowy pockets beneath the trees.

A mutter of satisfaction slipped from his lips. A road, traveled enough to be distinct, appeared beyond a tangled hedge of gooseberry bushes interlaced with other brush. Reaching it, he swerved hard right, and then after the wagon had leveled off, settled down. His face was grim, patched with sweat—and he knew he was taking a long chance; but they had to locate the road leading to Rolla.

Marcie, quiet all through the reckless ride down the slope, turned to him suddenly. "The supplies—we forgot them!"

"I know," he said. "Had to get out of there fast, and we're still not in the clear."

They would be passing, parallel, north of the settlement—just how close he had no way of knowing. He was gambling that Zurcher would send the soldiers he'd summoned toward the mill, never suspecting the object of the search to be moving in an opposite direction only a short distance away.

"But with no supplies—"

"We'll get by. Mules can do without grain for a couple of days."

He was oversimplifying it, he knew. The team needed rest, had been going all night in fact. He couldn't expect them to continue much longer—but they must keep at it until a safe distance from the town was reached.

A large building took shape through the trees to their right. The schoolhouse. The highway to Rolla would lie somewhere beyond it, according to what Gebhardt had told them. If they could draw close, again find a side road and proceed along it for a short time, the problem would be solved. Zurcher would not think of looking for them north of town.

An hour later he found what he sought, a shaded, well-screened coulee through which ran a small stream. There was ample grass for the mules, and they were close enough to the adjacent highway to hear passersby.

"From here all we need do is head north," he told Marcie as they climbed from the wagon.

She looked back toward Willow Grove. "Do you think we've gone far enough?"

"If they find us here, they'll find us anywhere," he said. "There anything left we can make a meal of?"

"I'll fix something," she said tiredly, and turned to the wagon bed. "Two more days. . . . I'll be glad when it's over with."

He looked at her. In the deep shadows of the trees he could scarcely make out her features. It would be strange going on without her. They'd been together for so long, been through so much. He'd miss Marcie—even if she had been the source of much trial and worry. He started to speak of it, but the words refused to come and he walked away, began to unharness the team.

They rested all that afternoon, and that night after the meal was over, he cut the cheesecloth he had purchased, and fortunately thrust into his pocket, into coverings for the mules. He'd remember to apply fresh mud in the morning before they pulled out, rubbing it deep into the burned-in letters and smearing it about thickly. This, combined with the netting, ostensibly used to ward off flies and other insects, should make the telltale identifications almost unnoticeable.

They were on their way early, following a trail of deep-cut wagon-wheel tracks that offered no advantage other than that it bore due north. The main road, to their right, continued to run alongside. Occasionally they heard the hard pound of galloping horses, and once when the two routes swung to close proximity, they caught the rattle of a wagon and the sound of voices.

They halted at another stream at midday, but only long enough to have a bite of lunch and rest the mules. The remainder of the daylight hours and the night passed without incident and Marshak concluded they had successfully eluded Zurcher and the soldiers he had called for.

Relief was short-lived. Not long after pulling out that next morning the road suddenly abandoned its adjacent course, swung to the right and joined with the main highway. Jeff, disturbed by the dangerous possibilities their presence on the primary route created, spent a half hour endeavoring to locate another alternate trail. He gave it up finally; steep hills lay to either side and it was evident there was no other way to Rolla.

Uneasy, he drove the mules onto the wide, hard-packed road. Immediately they began to encounter other travelers, both going to and coming from the city.

"Be lucky if we get through without being stopped," he said, his voice low with anxiety. "If we are—it's the same story we've been using."

Marcie Denton made no reply. He glanced at her sharply. "You hear?"

She only nodded and his concern heightened. Marcie could easily give it all away now, if she wished. He no longer had the vast reaches of empty land with which to intimidate her and bend her to his will. There would be soldiers about; she'd have no problem.

He leaned forward, letting the mules have their way. One advantage, they could move faster on the excellent road. They should reach Rolla before sundown if all went well. He mopped at the sweat on his face, shrugged off the tension that rode him; *if all went well.*

Marshak straightened warily as they rounded a short bend. A dozen blue-uniformed men were strung across the highway.

"Roadblock," he muttered hoarsely. "Zurcher sent word ahead.

Marcie drew up taut beside him, making no sound. He reached to the floorboard, pushed the Henry rifle under the seat, dragged a covering of blanket over it, then began to slow the mules.

A husky sergeant-major, flanked by two privates carrying muskets, moved forward of the line of soldiers in lackadaisical steps. The remainder of the squad continued to stand while off on the shoulder of the road two men assigned horse-holder duties waited with their charges. Pursuit, if he attempted to run the blockade, would be instantaneous, Jeff realized. His one hope was to bluff passage through.

Stiff, but managing a quizzical smile, he pulled the team to a stop. "What's the trouble?"

The bluff-faced old noncom advanced slowly, passing the mules without shifting his red-rimmed eyes. The privates separated, moving one to either side of the team.

"Who're you, mister?"

"Name's Castleman," Jeff said, using the name for a second time.

"Where you headed, Mister Castleman?"

Marshak pointed to the coffin. "Rolla. Aim to bury my brother there."

Silent, he watched the soldier scan both Marcie and him with close attention. Zurcher, if he had alerted the detail, would have given a description of them, but he had not seen the wagon or the mules.

"Where you from?"

Best to brazen it out, not come up with a name that could

be wrong—and they were on a road that connected the two settlements.

"Willow Grove."

He felt Marcie stir nervously. This was her opportunity if she intended to grasp it. She had but to speak a half a dozen words, and it would all be over. Tense, he waited while the sergeant-major stepped nearer the wagon, glanced at the items in the bed.

"Mind telling me what you're looking for?" Jeff asked, anxious to draw the man's attention.

The soldier drew back, dropped his head forward. "Happens there's a war going on," he said dryly. "Maybe you ain't heard about it."

Marshak nodded. "I've heard."

He must act casual, not betray the urgency within him that pressed for flight. Any such move would be fatal.

"You seen any riders in the hills wearing gray uniforms?"

"Rebs?" Jeff exclaimed, feigning surprise. "Around here?"

"Yep, around here—everywhere. Been reports of them sneaking in, working north. We're expecting trouble up Lexington way."

Apparently Zurcher's description hadn't been too good—or he and Marcie looked like many others who dwelt in the Ozark hills. He wagged his head.

"Sure ain't, Sergeant. . . . Never figured they'd try going through this part of the country."

The noncom spat in disgust. "Plenty of them. People in this here state can't seem to make up their minds what they want." He paused, looked beyond the end of the wagon. The beat of oncoming hoofs was a rapid sound on the warm air. He made a motion with his freckled hand.

"You people can go on through," he said, stepping back. "You see anybody looks like a Reb, get yourself to the first soldier you can find and report it. Understand?"

"Sure will," Marshak said, keeping his expression serious.

He slapped at the mules with the reins, sent them plunging forward into the harness. The privates jumped clear hastily, one of them grinning at Marcie as the wagon rolled by.

Jeff glanced back over the road. A buggy, drawn by two impatient blacks, was pulling to a stop at the blockade. Whoever it was he felt he owed them a debt of gratitude; they had arrived at just the right moment.

He turned to Marcie. "Want to thank you. Was afraid—knowing how you feel—you'd tell that sergeant—"

She lowered her eyes, toyed with a seam in her faded dress. "I had the thought."

"Figured you did. I'm obliged to you—more than I can say."

Marcie stirred. "We're so close—and it seems to mean so much to you. I—I couldn't do it."

"Means plenty to others, too," he said, and reached into his pocket. "Before I forget, want to give you this," he added, dropping several gold pieces into her hand.

She stared at the coins and then at him. "What's this for?"

"You'll need it for clothes and for your fare to Pennsylvania."

"I won't take your money."

"Not mine. Army issued traveling expenses to me, along with requisition forms. Lost them in the fire at Whiterock. Lucky I carried the money in a belt."

"But you've still got to get to Washington. You'll need money for that."

"There's enough."

They rolled on in silence for a time, and then Marcie said: "I think I owe you something, too. An apology for the way I've acted."

"Goes for both of us. Know I was a bit rough with you at times, but I was only doing what I figured had to be done."

Again the things he wanted to tell her pushed to the fore, and once more he found it impossible to give them voice. Later it would be easier, he assured himself.

But as the day wore on and Rolla at last came into view and the first outlying houses began to appear along the roadside, he felt a change come over him, and abruptly he was seeing it differently. He was a soldier—a man at war, perhaps with his own army if it turned out he'd be unable to clear himself of the charges with which he was certain to be faced.

He had no right to speak to Marcie; it would be unfair. And by what stretch of the imagination did he think his words would be welcome, anyway? He had seen hatred in her eyes more than once during the interminable hours that stretched between there and Fort Whiterock—and would not the specters of Jeremiah Denton and Carey Mossman stand forever between them?

He was a fool to think—Marshak's labored thoughts died and he came to swift attention. In the dark shadows of trees fringing the road in gatelike formation a quarter mile ahead, his eyes caught the brittle flash of silver in the slanting sunlight. Straining, he determined the blurred outlines of two horses.

Jeff swore savagely under his breath. Krause! He hadn't lost him after all! It could mean nothing else. The outlaws had swung wide, as he had thought they might do, laid their ambush in a most appropriate spot. . . . If the *vaquero*'s horse hadn't stirred, drawn attention to its silver-mounted saddle. . . .

He glanced at Marcie. The flash had gone unnoticed by her. Immediately he cut off the road, angled toward a small farmhouse where an elderly man and woman sat rocking on the porch, taking their ease in the waning afternoon.

The girl looked at him questioningly as he drew to a halt in front of the gate. "Why are we stopping here?"

"Don't think we ought to ride in together. If something goes wrong be better for you if you're not seen with me."

"But you'll need me more—" she said, doubtfully.

He took her arm, pushed gently. "Just do as I say."

She stared at him, baffled, and then climbed slowly from the wagon. "I—I don't understand."

"Best this way," he said, smiling. "These folks will get you to town." He ducked his head at the couple on the porch. They had ceased rocking, were watching with interest.

"Will I see you again?"

Somewhere in Rolla a locomotive hooted twice. "Maybe," he said, taking up the reins. "Never know who's standing around the next corner. Good-bye."

Marcie raised her hand. "Good-bye," she said quietly, her voice breaking slightly. "Good-bye, Jeff."

22

Marcie's voice was so low Jeff scarcely heard her words, but he was struck by the fact she had, for the first time, used his given name. He looked back, saw her standing near the fence, hand still lifted. Moving his arm he made his own responding farewell. He wished it could be different. Marcie Denton was a fine woman—a lot of woman, and one any man would be proud to call his own. . . . But she wasn't for him.

He placed his attention on the road and the grim moments that lay ahead. He wouldn't have Marcie to worry about now; he could meet the outlaws on even terms. Squinting, he studied the darkening trees. The point where he had seen the *vaquero*'s horse was a narrow entrance into what appeared a widely extending grove of large trees.

The perfect location for an ambush, he thought, and grinned tightly. Reaching down, he pulled his rifle from beneath the seat. Laying it across his knees, he cracked the mechanism and examined the chamber. The weapon was ready.

He looked around. There were no houses edging the strip of road ahead, and it was too shaded to tell if there were any within the grove; he hoped not, having no wish to see innocent bystanders struck by stray gunshots. . . . Krause would be on one side, he guessed, the Mexican on the other. They'd probably hit him just as he entered.

The locomotive whistled again, and a bell began to ring faintly. Be good if he could catch the train before it pulled out, but if he failed, there'd be another in a day or two probably. He'd as soon keep right on going, however.

Fifty yards. . . . Forty. The mules, tired and sensing the end of a day's work, moved along at a steady trot. Marshak hunched forward, hooked the reins on the whip-socket, leaving enough slack to please the team. Removing the whip, he eased back, and maintaining the level of his head and shoulders as much as possible, slid his legs, one after the other, over the seat until he was standing, crouched, in the wagon bed.

Tense, jaw set to hard lines, he held that position until he was no more than a dozen strides from the entrance to the grove. Then, lashing out at the team with the whip, he snatched up the rifle and threw himself full length beside the coffin.

The mules, startled by the unaccustomed treatment, threw their weight against their collars, broke into a dead gallop. The wagon began to sway from side to side, threatening to overturn, but Marshak gave it no thought. In the next moment the first of the trees sped by. He saw a dark shape step from the shadows. The *vaquero*.

Fading light flickered on the silver ornaments gracing his large, rolled-brim hat, glinted dully against the pistol in his hand. Jeff triggered a shot, levered, sent a second bullet into the outlaw. As the man staggered, began to fall, Marshak rolled, faced the opposite side of the road.

He saw the flash of Krause's weapon at the same instant wood splintered the edge of the seat. Jeff fired blindly at the orange splash in the depths of the brush, knew he had missed when Krause got off a second try.

The wagon whirled on, the mules crazed by the gunshots at such close range, racing at top speed. The deserter's bullet had dug a groove across the end of the coffin, thudded into the wooden sideboard beyond it. Marshak, striving to take aim at the outlaw's bent shape while the lurching wagon swept back and forth on the road, finally steadied himself. He caught the man in his sights, squeezed the trigger. Krause stiffened, spun half around, and fell.

The team was running wild and the dry, crackling sound he had sought to repair in the wagon's rear wheel was making itself heard again. Hanging onto the rifle, Jeff climbed back onto the seat. Bracing himself, he seized the reins, wrenched them free and began to haul back, all the while calling to the fear-struck animals. At first there was no response, and then the team began to slow.

The first of the homes lining Rolla's main street were rushing up to meet him. Several persons had come into the open, were standing in their yards or on the sidewalks staring toward the grove. A man dashed into the street, arms waving. Beyond him two soldiers, dressed only in boots, breeches and undershirts, were coming from a doorway.

"What's all the shooting?" the man shouted, still working his arms.

"Holdup—other side of the grove!" Jeff yelled as he sped by. "Scared hell out of my mules."

The man wagged his head sympathetically and Marshak allowed the mules to rush on, trying now to figure where the railroad would lie. The bell had stopped ringing, but a heavy streamer of black smoke hanging flat against the sky straight ahead seemed a good bet.

Guiding the mules around a corner he saw the central part of town directly before him. He swore softly, swung to his right at the next intersection. He had no wish to go thundering through the heart of Rolla. There would be soldiers and local lawmen, all of whom would wonder and undoubtedly give chase.

He caught sight of the train at the next corner, the stark, white letters, PACIFIC RAILWAY, showing plain on the dull black of the engine's tender. It was just getting underway, the engine belching steam from its pistons and smoke from the stack as it chuffed itself into motion.

Standing up in the wagon, Marshak endeavored to get a better view of the track. There appeared to be no road running parallel, only a wide ditch created when the grading was raised. It was too late to catch the train at the depot; he'd have to make his approach from the ditch, flag down the engineer from there.

He swung off the street, cutting across the unfenced yard of a startled resident, and dipped down into the excavation. The move placed him in front of the locomotive and immediately the engineer began to ring his bell, issuing a warning to clear the way.

The clatter and clamor set off the mules again. They began to fight the bit and for a short space of time Marshak feared they were going to overturn the wagon. The thunder increased as the locomotive drew abreast. Jeff looked at the engineer.

The trainman's face was beet-red. "What the hell's the matter with you? What're you doing down there?"

Jeff, gripping the reins with one hand, pointed to the coffin. "Got to take that to Washington. You get me there?"

The engineer shook his head, pointed to his ear, and reached in, throttled the machine to a smooth roll.

"You say Washington?"

Marshak bobbed. The mules were settling down.

"Why the hell didn't you get on at the station?"

"Tried—late. Got held up. How about it?"

The engineer shrugged. "Well, I don't go all the way, but we make connections," he said, pulling the string of cars to a grinding halt. He moved onto a lower step leading into the cab, watched as Jeff fought the mules to a standstill. A second man appeared behind him.

"Load into that third coach back," the trainman said, pointing a gloved finger. "Routed through to Philadelphia. You'll have to change there if it's Washington you're going to."

Jeff signified his understanding, began to back the rig toward the designated boxcar. He could see several heads sticking out of parlor coach windows, and two or three men had emerged and were standing on the grading.

The engineer moved aside, permitted the man behind him to drop to the ground. "Reckon you'll need a bit of help," he called. "Ernie'll give you a hand."

The car was half filled with sacks of grain. Ernie, a huge,

thick-bodied man who evidently tended fireman duties on the locomotive, helped Jeff slide the heavy coffin into the space between the evenly distributed load.

"Conductor'll be in the last coach," he said, returning to the grading. "Pay him."

Marshak reached into his pocket, drew out the last of his money. "Be glad to, but he'll have to come get it. I'm staying here—with my brother."

Ernie's brows lifted. "You aim to ride there all the way to Philadelphia?"

"All the way."

Up at the head of the train the engineer tooted impatiently. Ernie scratched at his chin. "Expect it'll be all right—and there ain't no rule against it. Conductor can do his collecting at the next stop. Sure is going to be a rough ride."

"Know that," Jeff said, "but I just don't want to leave here."

The engineer whistled again. Ernie started to turn away, pointed at the mules. "What about your rig?"

"Some of the family'll pick it up. They'll be along shortly."

The trainman trotted off, waving his arms to his chief as a signal to get underway. The locomotive puffed briskly, and as the startled mules whirled away toward a field to the side, a shudder went through the string of cars and they began to move slowly.

Jeff Marshak looked down at the sun-bleached, scarred coffin, sighed gustily. The worst was over. The long trip by wagon, the dangers, the hardships, Indians, Wade Krause—all were behind him—finished. Only Washington remained.

23

The morning was gray and the hint of a late summer rain hung in the sky when the train screeched to a halt in Washington station.

Jeff Marshak, leaner by twenty pounds, haggard from loss of sleep and lack of food, and looking more the frontier scout in his worn clothing, untrimmed beard and shaggy hair, rose from his seat on the coffin, and rolled back the baggage car door. Through eyes deep-sunk in their sockets, he peered out.

"Dray!" he croaked to one of the numerous wagons drawn up near the edge of the freight platform.

The man slumped in the light vehicle came alive, waved a hand in acknowledgment, and swung his wagon in alongside the coach. At this closer distance he had a second look at Marshak, and hesitated.

Jeff, sliding the coffin into the open doorway, raised up impatiently. "Grab a hold, goddamnit!"

The drayman hurriedly moved to his side, and together they wrestled the elongated box onto the vehicle. Marshak, taking up his rifle, resumed a position on the coffin.

"Capitol Building," he directed.

The driver's mouth sagged. "The Capitol?"

"What I said," Jeff snapped irritably.

The drayman, mumbling incoherently and shaking his head, returned to his seat. Gathering up the reins, he swung out onto one of the city's main avenues.

Streets and sidewalks were crowded, Jeff noticed. Businessmen, soldiers, politicians, laborers, and more soldiers—all were moving about in hurried, preoccupied silence. Manassas—or Bull Run, as he had discovered it was called in the North—had had a sobering effect upon the population and everyone appeared absorbed in preparation for the future.

Little had occurred since that initial clash between the two opposing forces, Jeff had learned from trainmen with whom he'd talked during the ride from Rolla. Washington officialdom had recognized their error in taking the threat of the South lightly, were gearing now to the sober business of fighting—and winning—an out-and-out war.

Lincoln had asked for more men, more money to provide needed equipment. Old Abe, as someone had termed the President, was roaring mad and didn't intend to get caught napping a second time. He'd even made changes in the Army command; General Scott no longer headed up the military. Those responsibilities now rested on the shoulders of a General McDowell—Irving McDowell. Scott was too old, and ailing. Better off retired.

Marshak had received that parcel of news with misgiving. Scott had been the one to countersign his special orders and he had looked forward to laying his military problems before the officer and asking his help in clearing them up.

But there was still the Secretary of the Treasury, Mr. Chase. He had written the letter of authority. Chase could help, although his influence in military matters would be limited. The long-standing hostility between the Army and political departments was well established and neither brooked interference from the other.

That, however, was something he'd worry about once he'd made delivery of the California War Chest, Jeff thought wearily. It had been a crushing weight on his shoulders for so long it would seem strange now to no longer feel its burden.

Just as it was odd to no longer see Marcie Denton sitting quietly at his elbow, giving him moments of anxiety, of anger and frustration. He wondered where she was by that hour—what she was doing. Safe and comfortable somewhere in Pennsylvania, no doubt. That was good. She deserved a rest.

"Whereabouts you want me taking you and that—that—"

The drayman's voice aroused Marshak. He looked up, aware of the stares of the curious along the avenue leading to the Capitol Building.

"Goes to the Secretary of the Treasury," he said, brushing exhaustedly at his eyes. "Don't know where his office will be."

The driver's gaze was fixed on the coffin. "You're taking that—a corpse—to him?"

"Know where to find him?" Marshak asked, ignoring the question.

The drayman shook his head. "Reckon it'll be in the main building. There's a side door, place where the trade usually makes deliveries." He paused, a doubtful expression on his wrinkled features. "Mister, you sure you want to do this?"

"Just take me to that side door," Marshak said, and lapsed into a torpid silence.

They swung into a narrow, side alley, continued along the massive, white building where a great number of persons were milling about on the broad steps, and pulled to a halt at a small landing. Three uniformed soldiers and a civilian sat on the edge. Their conversation ceased.

Marshak, pulling himself erect stiffly, reached into a pocket for a coin with which to pay the driver. "Let's get it off. I'll find somebody to help carry it inside."

The driver responded mechanically, and working together they hustled the coffin off the dray, onto the platform.

Jeff turned to the door. Pulling it back, he propped it open with a wedge of wood provided for the purpose, and glanced at the soldiers and their friend now standing around the box, looking first at him and then at the coffin.

"Goes to the Secretary of the Treasury—Mr. Chase," he explained. "Appreciate it if you'll give me some help."

The expressions of the four changed from wonder to amazement. The civilian was the first to find his voice.

"You crazy?" he asked incredulously.

"Sane as you are," Marshak snapped angrily. "Happens I'm under orders to—"

"Haul a corpse in there—dump it in Chase's lap—you've got to be some kind of a lunatic!"

Jeff Marshak's brittle temper snapped like a dry stick. Frustration swept through him in a surging wave. He whirled brought up his rifle, jammed the muzzle into the spine of the nearest soldier.

"Pick it up, God damn you!" he snarled, "or I'll blow you apart!"

Two of the men, a soldier and the civilian, leaned over hastily, placed their hands under the coffin. The Army man, sweat beading his face suddenly, threw a frightened look at his other companions.

"For God's sake, do what he says!"

They bent quickly, heaved the box aloft, rested it on their shoulders. Marshak prodded the soldier cruelly.

"Straight to Chase's office. . . . No tricks if you want to keep living."

The four men, staggering under their load, moved through the doorway into a long hall off which several doors opened. There was no one in the corridor, but at its far end where it led into a high-ceilinged lobby, Jeff could see a considerable crowd. Chase's office would be there somewhere, he guessed.

They reached the vaulted room, jammed with men, both in uniform and out, gathered in groups or scurrying about. The procession halted. Marshak pressed harder with the rifle.

"Keep going."

The soldier turned a strained face to him. "I—we don't know where—"

An officer wearing the insignia of a colonel suddenly cut away from a knot of men with whom he was speaking, and advanced in quick, staccato steps. His florid features were clouded.

"What's the meaning of this?"

Others turned to look and a gradual hush settled over the lobby. From near the front entrance two Marines began to move up.

Marshak's arm came up automatically in a stiff salute. "Captain Jefferson Marshak, sir, making a delivery to Secretary Chase—as ordered."

The colonel's eyes flamed. He glanced at the coffin, back to Jeff. "You crazy maniac!" he shouted. "How'd you get in here?" Wheeling, he beckoned vigorously to the approaching guards. "Arrest this madman!"

Marshak leaped back, leveled his rifle at the portly colonel's middle. "No—sir, not until I get this delivered. Nothing's going to stop me. . . . Try and I'll—I'll—"

He heard a sound behind him, tried to spin, but his jaded reflexes were too slow. A guard had moved in quietly, was swinging his musket. Jeff dodged, took a stunning blow across the head and shoulders. He felt himself going down.

"Turn him over to the provost marshal—and get that damned coffin out of here!"

The officer's voice seemed to be coming from a distance. Marshak was aware of strong hands grasping his arms, dragging him upright, propelling him toward the door.

Rage and desperation again boiled through him, lending him strength, clearing his fogged brain. He jammed his heels against the floor, whirled, threw one of his captors aside, drove his fist into the belly of the other. The deafening blast of a musket filled the room with echoes, and in that same fragment of time a monstrous, searing blow shocked his body and towering pain swept him into a vacuum of blackness.

24

The great hall was hushed when Marcie Denton entered. Neat and trim in a soft pearl traveling suit, dark hair capped with a jaunty hat, she was a small, striking figure caught in a shaft of afternoon sunlight streaming through the open doorway.

One of the Marines standing guard detail inside the building turned to look, interest breaking quickly in his eyes. He smiled and Marcie crossed to him.

"Corporal, the Secretary of the Treasury's office—can you tell me where it is?"

The Marine pointed to a hallway at the far end of the lobby. "Down that way, Miss. But nobody's there. All gone for a bite of supper."

"Will Mr. Chase be back, you think?"

"All depends. Sometimes him and the others work at night, sometimes they don't."

Marcie bit at her lips. The train had been late arriving—she had missed connection all the way from Rolla. It seemed her ill luck was to continue.

"There anything I can do for you, miss?"

"Maybe," Marcie said hopefully. "I'm looking for a friend. He would have been here yesterday, or perhaps the day before."

"People come—and they go."

"You'd have remembered him. Tall, probably still wore a beard and hair down to his shoulders. He wouldn't have taken time to fix himself—"

The Marine was looking at her closely, a puzzled frown on his face. "This friend—he have a coffin with him?"

"Then you saw him!" Marcie exclaimed. "Where is he? I've got to find him."

"The lunatic," the corporal muttered, and then nodded. "Yes'm, I saw him—saw him shot down, in fact. Happened right over there where—"

"Shot!" Marcie gasped, fear clutching her throat.

"Yes'm, shot."

Marcie was motionless for a long minute while everything within her slowly withered. In a dead voice she finally asked: "Do you know where they've taken him?"

"Try the provost's office in the old Capitol Prison. Expect they can tell you."

Numb, Marcie Denton murmured her thanks and returned to the street. Signaling a hack, she directed the driver to take her to the onetime seat of government, converted now to penal quarters.

The provost marshal was absent, also recessing for the evening meal, but a young officer appeared when she made her request known to the sergeant at a desk in the reception office.

"I'm Major Hale. You're asking about Captain Marshak?"

"Is—is he still here?"

The officer moved his head slightly. "You a relative?"

"Not exactly. We were—"

"I understand. Come with me."

Marcie trailed him into a short hallway at the end of which an armed guard stood at strict attention. Opening one of the two doors at the corridor's terminal, Hale stepped aside, admitted her into a large room filled with the pungent odor of antiseptic and the mutterings of men in pain. Rows of cots lined either side, and moving among them were several nurses and an elderly man in a white coat. Hale beckoned to the latter who presented himself wearily.

"This lady's asking about Captain Marshak, Colonel."

The surgeon smiled kindly, peered at the girl. "You wouldn't be Marcie?"

"Marcie Denton, yes. Did—did he speak of me?"

"Many times." The physician glanced to Hale. "I'll look after her, Major," he said, and taking Marcie's elbow, turned and started down the aisle separating the cots. "Bit crowded here, but we did the best we could for the Captain."

Marcie followed in stricken silence, only half listening. Nothing was clear in her mind, and she could find no courage to ask the questions that should be voiced.

The surgeon halted, pointed to a cloth screen closing off a corner. "In there."

Something caught in Marcie's throat, threatened to stifle her breath. She stared at the screen, whirled to the surgeon, but he was retreating down the aisle. Utterly alone then in the crowded room, she squared her small shoulders, hesitated briefly, and stepped into the enclosure.

Jeff Marshak, hair and beard neatly trimmed, lay in quiet composure on a bed next to the wall. He was a different Jeff Marshak from the one she had known, had journeyed untold miles and lived with for thousands of hours. His face was colorless, had thinned; eyes had receded deep into the skull and the hard, determined set of his mouth was gone.

Marcie lowered her head. "Oh, Jeff!" she moaned softly. "After all your work—your hopes—"

The man on the bed stirred. She looked up hastily, saw that his eyes had opened. A great rush of relief overwhelmed her, erupted in a flood of tears.

"You're alive—not dead!"

He mustered a weak grin. "Not quite. Guess I ought to be, from what the surgeon tells me."

"I thought—from the way everybody acted—"

Marshak shifted his body cautiously, extended his hand. "Come close. Got me all wrapped up, can hardly move."

Marcie hurriedly circled the bed, gripped his fingers. He was frowning.

"You didn't go to Pennsylvania?"

"No. After you left Rolla I decided to follow. Caught the train the next day."

"Glad you changed your mind. Kept missing you. Was always looking for you to be sitting beside me."

Marcie smiled. "Did everything turn out all right?"

He nodded, carefully and with effort. "Bit of trouble there at the last, but it worked out. Even got a letter from the Secretary thanking me." There was a touch of irony in his voice.

Again she smiled. "Now what happens?"

"They tell me I'll be here a couple more weeks. Then when I clear up the trouble I'm in—"

"I'll do that for you tomorrow. Afterward?"

"They'll be expecting me to report back in California. For duty."

"But in the meantime?"

A stillness came over Jeff Marshak. He stared at Marcie. "You wouldn't be thinking about marriage—us?"

"I would."

A smile of wonder spread across his lips. "Never thought you've even consider—"

"Oh, you're such a fool! Why do you think I came here, forgot Pennsylvania and everything else?"

"Didn't bother to think—was so glad to see you. It's settled then—want you to say it before you can change your mind; we're getting the job done soon as I'm on my feet."

Marcie tilted her head to one side. "The word of an officer and gentleman?" she asked mocking him deliberately.

"Officer and gentleman or not," Marshak said, reaching for her, "you can bet on it."